FINDING
THE
Magic

CAIT MILLER

ELLORA'S CAVE
ROMANTICA PUBLISHING

What the critics are saying...

ॐ

"Ms. Miller did it again with her second installment of her shape-shifter series, giving you a little more insight into the mysterious uncover group of shape-shifters, while interweaving mystery, action, and a sizzling love story that will curl your toes. [...] You will definitely find the magic within these pages, and though this is the second book, it isn't the last for Ms. Miller hints of a third story. Hopefully, it will be out soon. Highly Recommend!" ~ *Paranormal Romance Reviews*

3 Stars "This sequel may be enjoyed without having read Believe in the Magic, but it picks up seamlessly where the first book ends. Descriptive details are nicely drawn, creating a vivid canvas. [...] Plenty of interesting secondary characters leave the door open for more books in this series." ~ *Romantic Times Reviews*

4 Lips "Well written and intriguing *Finding the Magic* is a definite must read. Cait Miller does a superb job at character development, making you feel a part of their lives from the first page. With just the right combination of intrigue, action and romance this is a page turner. I am definitely looking forward to reading *Believe in the Magic* the other book in this series." ~ *Two Lips Reviews*

An Ellora's Cave Romantica Publication

www.ellorascave.com

Finding the Magic

ISBN 9781419957383
ALL RIGHTS RESERVED.
Finding the Magic Copyright © 2006 Cait Miller
Cover art by Syneca.

This book printed in the U.S.A. by Jasmine-Jade Enterprises, LLC.

Electronic book Publication October 2006
Trade paperback Publication March 2008

Also by Cait Miller

ॐ

Believe In the Magic

About the Author

❧

Cait Miller lives on the West Coast of Scotland in the same small town where she was born. She shares her home with a large collection of dragons and a miniature Yorkshire Terrier who has convinced the postman she's a Rottweiler. Cait dreams one day of living in a castle filled with history…or at least a house with a library.

Books and writing have played a huge part in Cait's life since she was very young. Encouraged by a mother with similar interests and one of the world's greatest English teachers, she began writing her own stories. Unfortunately she inherited a practical side to her nature from her grannie—who once told her at a party, in front of her teenage friends, to cross her legs not her fingers.

Cait went on to become one of the first people in her family to graduate from University where she trained for a medical profession. Writing became something she did for her own pleasure, never dreaming it could be anything else. Then, one day, she showed one of those stories to a group of online friends who taught her to Believe In The Magic…

If you are ever looking for Cait you only have to find the nearest quiet corner and she'll be there, book or pen in hand, wrapped up in another world.

Cait welcomes comments from readers. You can find her website and email address on her author bio page at www.ellorascave.com.

Tell Us What You Think
We appreciate hearing reader opinions about our books. You can email us at Comments@EllorasCave.com.

FINDING THE MAGIC

Dedication

‰

For the all women in my family who taught me everything I needed to know, as well as a few things I could have lived without knowing. Your courage, humour, wit and wisdom helped to make me who I am today.

With thanks to Kelly, who was my cheerleader; Patti, whom I couldn't punctuate without; Virginia, who pointed out the difference between strawberry sauce and honey; Renée, who nagged me until I finished; and Raelene for her unending patience and occasional cracking of the whip.

Trademarks Acknowledgement

‰

The author acknowledges the trademarked status and trademark owners of the following wordmarks mentioned in this work of fiction:

Technicolor: Technicolor, Inc.

Velcro: Velcro Industries B.V. Limited Liability Company

Glossary

Ceangal (Kea al) — Bond
Dearbh Ceangal (D′ earav Kea al) — Proven Bond
Fìor cèile (Fiar K′ ehli) — True mate
Sgian Dubhs (ski an doo) — traditional Scottish knife

Chapter One

∽

A cool breeze from an open window caressed her bare shoulders as she relaxed back into the shadows. Her lips parted on a soft moan of pleasure. Jayne Davis stretched her newly bared toes and kicked her confining high heels to the side. Relief. She'd been imprisoned in the silver shoes since early that morning. Had been fantasizing about the moment she could slip them off since dinner an hour and a half ago.

Floor-to-ceiling windows filled the wall on one side of the room and she knew the pair of doors in their center led out to a well-tended patio and garden. It had, so far, been unseasonably mild — for Scotland in January, that is. Thoughts of cooling her feet on the damp lawn posed a temptation she didn't think she could ignore. She wouldn't be able to stay outside for long dressed as she was but it would be lovely for a few minutes. The darkness outside reflected the room, making it seem larger than it actually was. The lights of the ballroom were designed to cast a soft glow on the parquet dance floor and give the seating areas privacy. This darkened booth in the corner seemed like the perfect place to hide away for a while and rest her aching toes.

Man, the things she'd do for friendship, she never was one for wearing skirts and dresses. In fact, she'd be surprised if there were more than a couple of each in her wardrobe. She much preferred the comfort of jeans, sweaters and sneakers. It had all but taken an act of God and some cleverly designed hidden support to get her breasts to stay where they were supposed to in this dress. Even then she was worried they might pop out of confinement if she should move the wrong way. Girlie clothes were more Megan's forte, Jayne rarely needed to dress up. On the surface she was friendly and outgoing but, truthfully, Meg was her only close friend. Jayne preferred to spend her free time losing herself in books where only the bad guys died and everyone lived happily ever after. Where magic was real and anything could happen.

She sipped her drink, savoring the sweet burn of the whiskey, and took in the scene before her. Her best friend stood in the arms of her new husband on the polished wooden dance floor, the ivory of her dress bright against Jack's dark suit. They had met less than four months ago when Jack had come from America to Scotland on business. Jayne still had no idea just what that business had been, but Megan and Jack had ended up running for their lives and had fallen in love. They swayed together, completely oblivious to the other couples around them and Jayne suppressed a sigh of envy. Since her father's death, she had guarded her emotions from all but Megan. Now, looking at the nauseatingly happy couple, she knew she wanted that to change.

She studied the groom with narrowed eyes. In a phone call a few months ago, Megan had urged Jayne to believe in magic. A few days before that her friend had asked her for advice because the man she'd just met thought he could turn into a cat. An understandably distraught Megan was convinced she had just had stupendous sex with a nutcase. It probably hadn't helped when Jayne's advice had been to give him the benefit of the doubt, Meg was remarkably narrow-minded when it came to the supernatural.

When they had next met, she had questioned her friend for details but Megan had merely smiled knowingly and shrugged her shoulders. All through Christmas Eve and Christmas Day, Megan had kept her silence. They had spent the whole of it together before she had joined Jack to celebrate with his family. Now here Jayne was at their wedding…and she was left with the strong suspicion that Jack be might more than he seemed. She smiled, realizing that her recent change of attitude had a lot to do with Meg's enigmatic statement. For the first time in a long time, she was noticing real life could be more interesting than fiction.

Speaking of which… Her gaze strayed over the rest of the guests. Less than forty in total. Although most of them were friends of the bride, she couldn't have imagined a more diverse group if she had tried. Nearby, Jack's parents were dancing, looking far too young to have a thirty-two-year-old son. All day, their happiness and pride in Jack had been evident to everyone. Regret flitted through her that neither Megan's nor her own parents were here. Her mother and Megan's parents had been killed when their car skidded on black ice and hit a bridge. A few years later the same bridge had claimed her father's life. She closed her eyes at the bitter memory, it was a bond both she and Megan could do without. A few nights ago, she and Megan had bought some wine and had a drink in their memory. Exchanging both happy and sad stories into the early hours of the morning and getting so drunk that Jack had come and put them both to bed. It had been an exorcism of sorts, a cleansing of sadness, allowing them to enjoy the wedding day with the renewed knowledge that their families would have wanted it that way.

On the edge of the dance floor, Danny, the Irish breakfast chef Megan worked with, was engaged in conversation with Meg's neighbor, Mrs. Timms. His brows were drawn in obvious puzzlement and his pint of beer was all but forgotten in his hand. The elderly lady had pulled out all the stops tonight with her pink taffeta dress. Perched on her pink-tinted hair, like a stuffed flamingo, was a large pink, feathered hat. Every now and then she directed a comment to the empty space beside her, causing one of Danny's fuzzy gray eyebrows to lift. Jayne chuckled, recalling her own first encounter with Mrs. Timms' long-deceased husband *George*. When she had nodded and politely introduced herself, Megan had looked at her as if she'd just stepped out of the twilight zone. Maybe the old lady was a little…*strange*…but in Jayne's opinion, just because they couldn't see George Timms didn't mean he wasn't there. She'd just never been able to convince her skeptical friend of that.

Her eyes continued to roam, passing over familiar and unfamiliar faces alike until they landed on the imposing form of Cameron Murray. He was standing at the bar, the overhead lights making his golden hair shine like a halo. She snorted at that. If there was anyone further from angelic in the room, Jayne had yet to meet them. His broad back was deliberately turned to her, as it had been most of the day. He was Jack's best friend and was supposed to be serving as his best man but, in her opinion, he wasn't doing a very god job of it. He hadn't shown up for any of the pre-wedding stuff—not even the rehearsal.

Megan had told her he was wealthy, that he lived in his family estate in the Highlands and that he ran a successful computer security company. The first time Jayne saw him was when she walked Jayne down the aisle. She had seen his shoulders tense and he had turned and glared, first at her then at an oblivious Jack. At the end of the ceremony, he had stalked ahead, leaving her to walk back up the church aisle unescorted. Since then, he'd avoided everyone, but most especially her, and that stung. Jayne couldn't think why she might want to attract the attention of someone as rude and unfriendly as him unless it was simply his physical appeal. He was certainly attractive, tall and broad through his shoulders and chest with a tight backside that she would love to get her hands on. His hair was blond and shoulder-length and his eyes were a wonderful golden brown that she'd love to see filled with heat, instead of cold and hard. *Shallow, Jayne, very shallow…*

Unlike Megan, who had described him to her as "a babe with a bad attitude", Jayne didn't think he was cover-model handsome but he certainly had a beautiful face. A square jaw, shadowed with golden stubble and a crooked nose that might have been aquiline at one time. He had a small scar on his chin and another through his left eyebrow. Something told her he could be a very dangerous man. One look at him and you could see he had lived and that it had been an eventful life, he *certainly* didn't look as though he sat behind computers for a living. Jayne's fingers itched for her paintbrush. Maybe it was time to retrieve her palette and easel from under the bed and brush the dust off. It was time to brush the dust off a lot of things, it seemed. She sighed and dragged her attention back to the dance floor.

* * * * *

She's watching me… Cam felt his whole body tense with the knowledge. He nursed a bottled beer and fought to keep his eyes focused on his fingers as they peeled the label off in strips. He had discovered her name was Jayne Davis and she had been a constant presence in his mind since he had seen her in the church this afternoon. He could feel her attraction to him but she didn't like him. He knew all he needed to do was look in the mirror behind the bar and he would see her sitting in the shadows. Her lips would be quirked in that annoying smile that seemed to say "I know what you're doing and I don't care".

He wanted her to care that he was ignoring her. It would only be fair. Already he was aware of her on a level he wouldn't acknowledge. His skin tingled and the air crackled with the magical energy that wanted to connect them. It was intense, like every cell of his body had suddenly come alive and become sensitive to her presence. The urge to go to her was so strong that he had to grit his teeth against it. He refused to consider that it could be anything more than the usual demand of the mating cycle. A demand that he had every intention of ignoring.

An image of her long slender body wrapped in her gray silk dress mocked him. The material clung to her curves from her breasts to her ankles, concealing the paw-shaped birthmark that he now knew had to be there. The light color made her upswept red hair burn like fire. How long was it?

Was it as soft as it looked? He wanted to release it from the clip that secured it and tangle his fingers in it. His cock hardened painfully and he shifted his hips, trying to relieve the pressure. "Shit." His soft exclamation drew the attention of the man standing next to him, and Cameron glared at him until the man tossed his drink back and walked hastily away from the bar.

Why hadn't Jack warned him? *Probably afraid you'd refuse to come...* He glanced over at his friend, he looked happy for the first time in more than a year. Cam wanted no part of it. He'd seen how bonded mates could destroy each other. Jack knew it too and yet, here Cam was, under the scrutiny of a woman who could make him forget. He had doubted that such a thing as a true bond even existed until he had been in the same room as her. It didn't change anything though. Even a *Dearbh Ceangal* doesn't guarantee happiness. Only torments you with the possibility of it.

Occasionally, Jayne's thoughts tracked through his brain, each one putting another dent in his resolve not to acknowledge her. She thought him rude and arrogant. That didn't bother him. It was a popular opinion, though most people were afraid to express it. It didn't make any difference that she thought he wasn't worth her time.

Really.

He tipped his bottle to his lips in an attempt to ease his dry throat and almost choked as she turned her attention to his backside. It couldn't hurt to introduce himself, could it? Just to show her he wasn't as worthless as she believed? Her intention flitted through his brain an instant before she moved and he watched her reflection weave its way toward the patio doors at the far side of the room. The gray silk of her dress dipped dangerously low at the back, revealing a small henna tattoo in a Celtic design at the base of her spine. Throwing a couple of banknotes beside his abandoned drink, he followed her, suddenly glad that he was the only unmated shifter in the room.

Beyond the lights of the patio, the partial moon gilded the trees and shrubs with a white luminescence. The air was cold and Cam could smell snow on the light breeze, along with the light, spicy scent of her perfume. Jayne stood in the middle of the neatly trimmed lawn, her shoes dangling from her fingertips. A slight smile curved her lips and her face was tilted toward the clear sky, her eyes closed as though she was being bathed by the sun instead of moonlight. She looked ethereal, like a fey queen with her creamy skin and fiery red hair and, for a moment, he was frozen. Gradually the muted sounds of music and laughter from the ballroom intruded and he mentally shook himself, feeling ridiculous. When did he get so poetic? He cleared his throat, suddenly unsure how to approach her. The smile fled and she opened her eyes and looked at him. "What do you want?"

You, the thought rose instantly in his mind and he clamped his lips against the urge to say it. He crossed the wet grass until he stood in front of her. "To apologize, I shouldnae have ignored you…at the church." Her light eyes shone with mocking amusement.

"Just at the church?" she prodded.

"Aye."

She laughed. "Not the most tactful of people, are you? Don't worry, I'm sure I'll get over it." She turned her back to him and started to walk away and he caught her wrist. Her pulse fluttered under his fingertips like a trapped bird and he knew she wasn't as calm as she pretended to be. A gentle tug brought her around to face him, her hand resting on his chest. The contact burned his skin through his shirt. Arousal rushed through him, bringing his cock to full, painful attention, and standing as close as she was, he knew she must feel it too. Her confidence had fled, leaving behind uncertainty to battle with the desire in her eyes. Without conscious thought, he caressed her face with his fingertips, tracing the smooth, cool skin. She shivered and her lips parted on a shaky sigh.

"I told myself I wasn't goin' to touch you..." Cupping her head in his hand, he kissed her. Gently at first, just a sampling of her soft lips, then deeply, tasting the sweetness of the liqueur she had been drinking earlier. Dimly, he heard the thud, thud of her shoes slipping from her hand. His pulse pounded in his ears and his groin throbbed when she moaned and clutched at his shirt. Faint echoes of her desire mingled with his swirled through his head. Cam knew that, with a little focus, he could join her mind with his. Instinct hammered at him, *take her...take her...* He felt electricity crackle through his body and his fingertips began to tingle where he still grasped her wrist. Suddenly the significance of what he was feeling pierced the fog of desire. He pushed himself away from her, gasping, "No!"

She stared at him, bewildered, fingers pressed to lips that were swollen and wet from their kiss. His hands clenched into fists against the need to pull her back and finish what they had started, but the energy that still pulsed though him told him how close he'd come to doing what he'd sworn never to do. "Jayne, I—"

She held up a hand. "No, not another word. I need to get back inside before I'm missed." Cam watched as she scooped up the silver shoes and walked quickly back toward the patio, this time he made no move to stop her.

Jayne stared at her reflection in the gilt mirror in the ladies' room. Muffled music from the band was just audible through the closed door and the room behind her was empty. She hardly recognized the woman who looked back, her fingers tightened on the edge of the white porcelain sink. The light green eyes were hers but they held an excitement and a passion that had been missing since her father had died four years ago. A pink flush stained the fair skin of her cheeks and her red hair had come free in places from its silver clasp. It tumbled around her face, the ends brushing the bodice of her dress. Her nipples pebbled against the soft silk of her gown in a deliciously obscene way. She looked like a woman who had just been ravished.

She smiled as she thought about the man who had done the ravishing. Cameron Murray wasn't quite as aloof as he pretended and, in his hands, neither was she. For a moment in the garden, both of them had forgotten about keeping their distance and the result had been stunning. It had seemed that the very air around them had been electrified, sensitizing her skin to his touch. When he had kissed her, she had felt like she might come just from the feel of his lips and his tongue dancing with hers. It had been obvious from the hard feel of him pressing against her belly that he had felt the same. For those few seconds, something within her had reached toward him and she had wanted him to take it, more than she had ever wanted anything in her life.

Then he had stopped.

She frowned. He had thrust her away from him as though she had burned him. Why? Jayne shook her head. Whatever his reasons were, it wouldn't really matter. If he was as reclusive as Megan had implied, then it was unlikely she would see much of him. The kiss had been a good wake-up call for her hormones and she was grateful to Cameron for that. She slipped her feet back into her shoes, fixed her hair and smiled at her reflection. She would never stroke his ego by telling him so though.

* * * * *

Cam finally caught up with the bride and groom as they headed from the dance floor toward the shadows at the back of the ballroom. It had taken him a long time to get his body back under control and even longer to convince it that he didn't need to go after her. Even now, he could feel Jayne nearby and had to fight to ignore her. The couple stopped as they noticed his approach and Jack smiled at him. "Ah, busted! We were just about to sneak away…" His voice trailed off and he pulled Megan closer as he noticed Cam's scowl. "What's wrong?"

"Why didnae you tell me, Jack?"

Jack frowned at him. "Tell you what?"

"That she was one of the marked? You know how Ah feel about this and yet you brought me here without so much as a warnin'."

Understanding dawned in his friend's face and he shook his head. "I didn't know, Cam. I've never even met most of these people."

"Ah'm talking about Jayne!" he growled, his Scottish brogue becoming more pronounced.

Jack gaped at him, clearly astonished. "I had no idea, Cameron, I swear it. I was already linked to Megan when I met her for the first time. I knew she felt different, familiar...I just thought I was picking up Meg's feelings. I wouldn't recognize one of the marked now if they came up and shook me by the hand. You know that!"

He did know that. Once mated, the telepathy that helped his kind to recognize one of the marked existed only between the mated pair. Jack was telling the truth, he could feel the sincerity and surprise radiating from his friend. Megan, on the other hand... He speared Jack's uncharacteristically silent mate with his eyes and she flushed guiltily. "It's uh, how our mothers met." She winced when Jack swore softly.

"We were on the beach and they noticed we had the same birthmark and started talking. Some coincidence, huh?" Cam glared at her and Megan reached out to lay her hand on his arm before continuing quietly, "I'm sorry, Cameron. I didn't say anything because Jack wanted you to come and I didn't think you would if you knew about Jayne. I knew you didn't want a mate and since you were going to be the only shifter here besides Jack's parents, I thought it, she, would be safe."

"She is safe, dammit!" There was a beat of heavy silence. Cam drew a deep calming breath and looked at the somber faces of his friends. "Look, nae harm done, but Ah think it's best if Ah leave now." He stepped forward and kissed Megan's cheek, then shook Jack's hand and drew him into a back-slapping hug. Despite the worry in their eyes, he walked away from them and out of the ballroom, feeling all the while that he was leaving a part of himself behind.

Chapter Two

ༀ

The feeling was still with him two days later as Cam paced restlessly in front of his second-floor office window. Ordinarily, the view helped bring him peace and today it was particularly spectacular. The sun was just rising over the hill and it lit the scene with a fresh, golden light, turning darkness into lengthening shadows. There had been a light fall of snow overnight and the thin layer on his wide lawn was pristine and undisturbed. It dusted the pine forest that surrounded his family home like a layer of confectioner's sugar. Just beyond the trees at the base of the hill, he could see part of his small loch, as still and smooth as a mirror. There wasn't another house in sight, though he knew that there was a small village just a couple of miles away, nestled in a sheltered valley. The undisturbed land around him usually gave him a sense of freedom and safety. Today it just felt isolated.

Since he had left the wedding reception and Jayne Davis behind, nothing had given him respite. The little sleep he had managed to grab had been filled with the kind of erotic dreams that would put a porn star to shame. When he woke, his cock was as hard as steel and not even an ice-cold shower or taking matters into his own hand had relieved it for long. He just needed to get her out of his mind. Unfortunately, with the information he had discovered this morning, it didn't look as if that was going happen.

The computer hummed softly behind him, the database he had been studying covered by a screensaver. Its animated image of a man transforming into a house cat caught his eye. He watched it cycle through a couple of times, remembering the first day it had flickered on. Nick Douglass had hacked into the machine. Hiding the program in the hard drive just to prove he could. Nick had thought it was hilarious that he had been able to outsmart him, the "computer security expert". Cam had tried for over a week to get rid of it with no success. He had fully intended to threaten Nick with bodily harm if he didn't fix it when he came to Scotland. Only his friend hadn't arrived.

He had finally figured out how Nick had done it but he didn't want to delete it anymore. That stupid animation had become a memorial to Nick. A reminder that it was up to Cameron to find out what had happened to him. After all, if he hadn't refused to go and pick him up at the airport eighteen months ago... He closed his eyes in regret. He knew Nick had arrived at the airport since he had collected his rental car. He even had the surveillance tapes of the garage to prove it. The car had been found abandoned and empty on a country lane about twenty miles away from Murray House. No one had heard from him since and, until recently, there had been no new leads.

When Jack and Megan had come to him for help, he had set out to find the identity of the person trying to kill them. Unable to find any motive for getting rid of either of them, he had looked for similar crimes. He found that a number of shapeshifters had disappeared over the last couple of years, Nick Douglass was one of them. At the time, they had been looking for mated couples who had vanished and, in the end, he had dismissed them as unrelated. The disappearance of the others had continued to bother him though.

When they had finally caught up with James York, the man who had been trying to kill his friends, Cameron had found that the man had extensive notes on shapeshifters. He must have gotten that information from somewhere and Cam couldn't help but wonder if it had anything to do with the missing shifters. He might just be grasping at straws but anything that might help him find out what had happened to Nick was worth checking. With this in mind, he had continued to investigate.

This morning, he had made one of his periodic checks of the missing persons' database to check for further disappearances. There had been one new entry, a twenty-three-year-old woman, and listed under identifying characteristics was a very familiar birthmark. It had only taken him seconds to discover that she wasn't the first. In fact, two other women bearing the cat's paw birthmark had been reported missing in the last three months. It appeared that whoever else was targeting shapeshifters had decided to include the marked. Fear and anger had filled him as he realized that Jayne might be in danger.

So now here he was, pacing like a caged lion, trying to figure out how to protect her without taking her. Joining her mind and soul to his was what his every instinct screamed he should do. He knew she was alone, her parents were gone, both killed in car accidents. She was single and everything he had been able to find out told him she had few close friends. Cam had plenty of contacts so it would be easy to find someone to guard her, but he couldn't bring himself to pick up the phone. It was like some great, big cosmic joke. The very thought of another man laying his hands on her in any way was intolerable. It left him with only one other option, to go himself. He just hoped his willpower was up to the challenge.

* * * * *

Jayne turned the last page with a sigh of pleasure. She always had mixed emotions on finishing a really good book. Sadness that the story was over and satisfaction that the characters had gotten their happy ending. She leaned back into the plump pillows of the sofa and basked for a moment in the warmth of the sun shining through the windows. She wished she could make this feeling last forever. If she closed her eyes, she could almost believe it was summertime. Unfortunately, she had to go to work this afternoon. That meant she would have to leave the illusion behind her and face the cold winter's day that it actually was. It had been snowing overnight but not heavily enough to defeat the salty air of a seaside town for long. On top of that, the sun had come out this morning and, as a result, the snow had turned to a muddy slush. Jayne grimaced at the thought of walking through it.

The jangling of her doorbell interrupted her reverie. Jayne sighed and, for an instant, considered ignoring it, but she couldn't do it. She was too curious. She brushed her long straight hair over her shoulders and back from her face and went to answer it. It could only be a salesperson, she couldn't think of anyone else who would be at her door. Her brows pulled down in a frown. Now that was sad. How had she managed to cut herself off so completely? It hadn't been intentional, it had just sort of happened.

She had been on the right track the other night at the reception. It was time to take back her life. Kissing a man in a moonlit garden had been a good start. The memory of that kiss had occupied her thoughts for a good portion of the last few days. Even now she shivered with remembered sensations. She needed a man. Bob, her vibrating friend, just wasn't doing it for her anymore. She could almost hear Megan cheering from here. She was lifting her hand to unlock the door when the bell sounded again. Whoever it was wasn't the patient sort.

"Whatever you're selling, I'm not..." her voice trailed off, fingers tightening on the handle of the door. She blinked in astonishment at the man standing in her doorway. He was dressed casually in a dark sweater, faded blue jeans and a brown suede jacket. His jaw bristled with stubble and golden hair fell in disarray to his shoulders. She felt instantly frumpy in her jogging pants, bulky sweater and stocking feet.

"Cameron?"

He scowled at her and, fleetingly, she wondered if it was because she'd used his first name. She dismissed the thought as ridiculous. Mr. Murray was a little too formal for someone who had had his tongue in your mouth. Scowling just seemed to be his default expression, he did it a lot.

"What are you doing here?"

No sooner were the words out of her mouth than it occurred to her that there was only one explanation for him being here. Her heart thundered.

"Megan and Jack...are they..." she couldn't make herself finish the question. His brows raised in a brief expression of surprise.

"They're fine."

Relief swept through her. She couldn't have handled it if she'd lost Megan, too. She studied the taciturn man in front of her in confusion.

"Then why are you here?"

He moved toward her and she was captivated by the restrained power of his body. Unconsciously, she stepped back, opening the door for him. He strode past her without answering, heading unerringly toward her living room. Jayne shook her head and closed the door behind him.

He was standing by the living room window, hands in his jeans pockets, when she caught up with him. His scowl had been replaced by a pensive frown.

"Care to tell me what you're doing here?" She sat on the arm of one of the armchairs and watched him. He stood completely still, yet he seemed to fill the room with his presence. There was something about him that drew her and yet, at the same time cautioned her to stay away. She wasn't afraid of him, though he could undoubtedly be a dangerous man. The air around him fairly vibrated with it.

He abruptly shifted his attention from the window, pinning her with his amber gaze. Jayne stared back patiently and waited.

"I'm here because you're in danger."

She wasn't sure what she had expected him to say but it definitely wasn't that.

"Danger?" she repeated doubtfully. "From what?"

"You know about the man who was after Jack and Megan?"

She nodded. "He had some kind of grudge against Jack. What does this have to do with me?"

"Somebody told James York where to find them, gave him details about their lives. I believe that person might come after you next."

"Why?"

"I don't know why yet," he growled and swept a hand through his hair. "I dinnae even know *who*. I only know there have been other, similar cases where someone like you has disappeared."

"What do you mean someone like me?"

He was silent a moment. "Someone with the same…characteristics as you."

He glanced out the window again, tension visible in every line of his body. Jayne had the impression he would rather be anywhere but here. The fact that he had believed strongly enough that she was in danger to come here to warn her made her more inclined to take him seriously.

"Shouldn't we go to the police?"

"No! I…there's no evidence I can take to them."

Jayne blinked in surprise at the vehemence of his reply. "Well…okay. I'll take care…" he took a step toward her and she trailed off.

"No' good enough."

The statement brought her to her feet, wiping away her calm façade. "What do you mean 'No' good enough'? What else do you want me to do?"

"I want you to come home with me back to Murray House. Now. I can protect you there."

He had the most amazing voice, even when he was growling at her. Wickedly deep and smooth, it was an unusual mixture of American and Scottish. It poured over her like melted dark chocolate. Unbearably tempting. For a second, part of Jayne yelled, *Yes*! But sanity prevailed, for once. "No. I'm sorry but, no." *You have no idea how sorry.* "I can't just up and leave everything at a moment's notice. I have a job."

"Is it more important than your life, lass?"

"You don't even know for sure that my life is in danger!"

"Nevertheless, you *will* come with me." He glared at her, hands clenched at his sides.

Jayne laughed. "Don't you pull that 'Lord of the Manor' shit with me, Cameron Murray. You might have more money than God but that doesn't give you the right to order me about."

He studied her in silence, expression thunderous. A muscle ticked in his tightly clenched jaw and she had the impression that he was fighting some internal battle.

"Fine," he ground out. "Then Ah'll stay here."

Jayne tilted her head, considering. She wondered if he was aware that his Scottish accent thickened when he was mad. What else would bring out the Scot in him? Lord, he was a wonderful specimen, even when he was pouting. What would she give to see that powerful body naked? Every one of her hormones stood up and screamed at her, *"Do it, Jayne!"* She thought of Bob, her trusty but weary friend. Hadn't she decided just this morning that she needed a real man? Why not this one? Her flirting skills might be a bit rusty after all this time but she could at least try. Her chances would be increased tenfold if he were under her roof for a few days until he was convinced she was safe.

After all, he was kind of a friend of the family and he had driven all the way from the north of Scotland to warn her... It just wouldn't be right to just send him straight back, now would it? There was something about Cameron Murray that had instincts she thought she had lost twitching back to life. It was just the kind of impulsive decision the old Jayne would have made and, if she was going to take back her old life, what better way? She smiled at him and he met her eyes with suspicion.

"Okay."

Cameron blinked in surprise at her easy compliance. He had been prepared for an argument and was aware of a vague feeling of disappointment that she hadn't given it to him.

"You agree?"

She nodded serenely and he frowned at her suspiciously. She was up to something. He hadn't picked up any specific thoughts, but he was sensing a kind of muted anticipation and excitement from her. He watched as she stood up and started toward the sitting room door.

"Make yourself at home, the sofa in the library folds out into a bed. I have to go to work so I'll see you when I get back this evening."

He shook his head and followed her down the hall, leaning against the wall outside her bedroom. Drawers opened and closed and he tried not to imagine what she was doing. Against his will images of Jayne naked drifted into his mind. He wondered if her skin tasted as creamy as it looked. He wanted to nibble and lick his way up those long legs, run his tongue over the birthmark that proclaimed her his. Did she have freckles? There were none on her face but that didn't mean they were absent from her body. Were her nipples pale pink or soft peach? Given her hair color, he thought they would probably be pink. He pictured them peeking through that hair as it hung loose and free over her shoulders. Tangling around them both as she straddled him. Would her fiery red pubic hair burn him when he entered her? Or was she bare? Cameron moaned as his cock surged to eager life. *Stop it*! *Stop torturing yourself, you bloody idiot*!

The door behind him opened and Jayne sailed past him, dressed now in black trousers and an ugly green shirt. Her hair tied back, hanging in a long ponytail down her back. She seemed completely oblivious to his presence. She had put him out of her mind, her thoughts now filled with her job. He didn't like the fact that she might be able to do that when he was struggling to do the same. Heels clicking on the hardwood flooring, she walked to the hallway closet and pulled out a black coat. He reached for her, shackling her wrist with his hand, angry green eyes snapped at him but Cameron paid them no mind. The instant he touched her, every thought vanished from his head and all he was aware of was the softness of her skin and the warm pounding of her pulse beneath it. She pulled out of his grip and shrugged into her jacket.

"I have to go to work."

Shaken by his reaction to just that small touch, it was a moment before he responded. "I'm going with you."

She chuckled, shaking her head. "No, I don't think so."

"You need to be protected."

"Cameron, I understand that you're concerned but I'm only going to work. In a supermarket, not a combat zone. Though, admittedly, it can feel like it when the sales are on. I think I'll survive."

"No, Jayne, I dinnae think *you* understand. These people, whoever they are, dinnae play around. The missing people I told you about were all taken when they were alone, going about their daily lives. No warning, just gone. No trace of them has been found. I am going with you. Besides, it's a public place. You cannae stop me."

He followed as she turned her back to him and marched out the door. "Fine," she muttered through clenched teeth. "But if you get me fired..." Her threat trailed off ominously and Cameron's teeth flashed in a rare smile. She was...a challenge.

Chapter Three

ॐ

Jayne handed the credit card and receipt back to her customer with a smile that faded the instant the woman walked away. For about the hundredth time since she had sat down at the checkout point, her gaze drifted toward the wide storefront window. Yep, he was still there. His blond hair shone in the patch of sunlight where he stood, leaning against the wall of the building across the street. Watching her with unnerving intensity.

She had ignored his presence as she walked to work, pretending she couldn't feel him just behind her all the way. While she marched through the shop to the staff room, he had prowled through the shop, looking, she assumed, for any threat. Then with a long heated glance, he had walked out of the store and across the street to stand with what looked like endless patience in his current spot. Jayne swore that every female in the place had sighed longingly as the door had shut behind him. Including herself.

He nodded at her and she looked away quickly. Searching for a distraction in the now quiet store, she was relieved to see Linda approaching from the direction of the manager's office. There was a sympathetic expression on her colleague's face. It was enough to tell Jayne she was not going to like whatever Mr. Harrison had said. The little weed.

"Jayne, I know it's a hassle but the boss wants you to switch places with me and work in the stockroom today. I'm really sorry."

And she was. Linda knew as well as she did just why Frank wanted her there.

Privacy.

Jayne had thought—no, *hoped*—that her threat of sexual harassment charges had been enough to finally discourage him. He hadn't touched her since then. She should have realized it wouldn't last, creeps like him never changed. It wasn't a route she really wanted to take, it would probably mean losing her job. They couldn't fire her for it, even if he was the owner's son. She doubted she could continue to work here though. Much as she hated to admit it, Harrison was right. There was a stigma attached to anyone who involved themselves in a sexual harassment case. With a sigh of resignation, she logged off the cashier system.

The stockroom was essentially a large warehouse almost as big as the shop itself. It had a full-sized roll-up door in the rear so that the delivery trucks could be unloaded with ease directly into it. One half was filled with rows of floor-to-ceiling shelves packed with boxes, while the other was taken up by a refrigerated room and a huge freezer room. Jayne hated those and avoided them at all costs. As large as they were, she still felt claustrophobic in them. Both were sealed with large heavy doors and, although she knew they could be opened easily from the inside, she had a fear of being trapped in them. She turned her back on them determinedly and grabbed the clipboard with the inventory list from its hook on the wall. Linda had only checked off the first few items so it was easy to find where she had left off and, within a few moments, Jayne was absorbed in the task.

She had just reached the end of the first page when she began to feel as though she wasn't alone. The back of her neck prickled with awareness and the scrape of a shoe on concrete confirmed it. With deliberate casualness, she sat the clipboard on top of the box she had been checking and turned, unsurprised to find Frank Harrison behind her, just a few feet away. Damn, but the man could move quietly when he felt like it.

He was average height, which made him about an inch shorter than Jayne, more if she wore heels. Which of course she did, just to annoy him. Average build, mid-brown hair, brown eyes, not handsome, not ugly. He was dressed in a mid-range gray suit with a white shirt and a dark blue striped tie. Everything about the man's appearance was just average. The only thing that set Frank apart was his personality. His total belief was that he was God and everyone else—especially women—were put on this earth for his amusement.

"Mr. Harrison, is there a problem?"

He walked toward her, a slight smile on his face. "Now, Jayne, I thought we had progressed beyond last names. Haven't I told you to call me Frank when we're alone?"

Yeah, right. Jayne watched him warily, resisting the impulse to take a step back when he invaded her personal space. He'd love that, a sign that he threatened her. "I'd rather not, Mr. Harrison."

His smile broadened. "Well, maybe I can change your mind." The thick, cloying smell of his aftershave drifted around them, making it all the more difficult to stand her ground. She frowned as his muddy brown eyes drifted down the length of her body then returned to fix on her breasts. *Okay, that does it.*

"Mr. Harrison, you are making me uncomfortable. I meant what I said before about taking action against this kind of behavior."

He shook his head and laid his hands on the curve of her waist. "I think we both know you're not going to do that, Jayne. If you were, you'd have done it already."

"You know, you're right." And the knowledge grated, what kind of coward had she turned into? She straightened to her full height. "But I have decided that I don't need this job enough to put up with you. I quit." His eyes widened at the steel in her tone and made her smile, it was a tone he had never heard from her before. "I haven't decided yet whether to press charges against you but…you know that little place in my letter of resignation where you put reason for leaving…? Now, take your bloody hands off me." Anxiety flickered briefly over his face before he could hide it. Jayne took a step forward, smile broadening when he stepped back.

He shoved his hands in his pockets and regarded her warily. "You owe us two weeks' notice."

Jayne's eyes narrowed dangerously. "True, and you owe me four weeks' holiday pay…but hey, you know I'm not afraid to work. I'll finish the two weeks before you pay me the four weeks you owe me. It'll give me a chance to chat with the rest of the girls. Explain the situation to them…"

Jayne watched as her implied threat registered. He might be able to sweep one lawsuit for sexual harassment under the rug but not half a dozen.

"I see. Well, perhaps, under the circumstances, it would be agreeable if we were to count your holiday time as your notice. It would mean of course that you would need to leave now."

She resisted the urge to roll her eyes as he danced around the issue. "That works for me. Of course, if one of the girls was unhappy in the future, the situation might change."

He glared at her and gave a sharp nod before turning and heading for the door. "I'll expect your keys on my desk within the hour, Miss Davis."

Jayne flipped the bird at his retreating back and when the door clicked shut behind him she threw victorious fists in the air. "Yes! I am back!"

The sound of a lone pair of hands clapping made her whirl toward the shadows at the back of the room. Cameron. His expression held the remnants of anger and a grudging respect as he walked slowly toward her. He dropped his hands to his sides and nodded toward the door. "Nicely done."

She shrugged uncomfortably. "It was past time. How long have you been standing there?"

"Long enough to know that if he'd touched you again, Ah'd have broken his fingers." He made the statement so matter-of-factly that she knew he was utterly serious. It reminded her again that this man could be very dangerous if crossed. But not to her, she was certain of it.

"Well, thanks, but I was doing just fine on my own." Reality was finally sinking in. She had just become one of the unemployed masses, a first for her. *God, Jayne, when you decide to change your life you don't wait around. What now?* She studied the man in front of her. His large, silent presence was strangely comforting. *Why not?* She ignored the little voice in her head that urged her to retreat back to her flat and the escapism offered by her library. It was time to take the kind of risk she had been hiding from. The kind of risk she had urged her best friend to take a very few months ago.

"I think I've just been hit head on by destiny," she muttered.

"What?"

"Nothing. Well, I seem to have some time on my hands." He didn't comment, just watched her with his an almost predatory stillness and anticipation in his golden-brown eyes. As though his prey was in sight and it was only a matter of time before it —*she*—was in his grasp. *Come on, Jayne, take the plunge.* It should have been frightening but instead, it made her body flush with the heat of arousal. Seven years ago she wouldn't have hesitated, but that was before she let grief and fear take over her life. He wanted her to go with him and whether she believed she was in some kind of danger or not, wasn't it better to be safe rather than sorry? *You're rationalizing, Jayne, but so what.* She looked at this big, enigmatic stranger and the old Jayne saw adventure there. He had secrets and the anticipation of finding out what they were made her feel...alive.

"So, what are the Highlands like at this time of the year?"

Cameron released the breath he hadn't been aware he was holding, unsure whether he had won the battle or not. He had felt her indecision, heard it in the few thoughts he had picked up. She had agreed to come home with him but he wasn't sure anymore that it was a good idea. The pull between them was becoming stronger the more time they spent together and it didn't seem as if Jayne had any intention of resisting it. Yes, she would be safer under his roof. But would he?

She ignored the curious glances of her colleagues as they walked through the store, stopping only to explain to the dark-haired girl who had replaced her at the checkout. Cam doubted anyone but he could tell she was anything other than calm and relaxed. But he had seen her hesitate before leaving the storeroom, straightening her shoulders and pulling a cloak of serenity around her. It had been difficult not to go to her and wrap his arms around her but he didn't trust himself. Instead, he only followed as closely behind her as he dared. Offering what support he could while she picked up her coat and bag and dropped the keys on the desk in the deserted manager's office.

She had said very little to him as they walked back to her apartment, other than to ask how long a trip to pack for. An answer he had been unable to provide. But instead of fuming at him, Jayne had merely shook her head and smiled wryly and he had felt her resigned amusement. Now he leaned against the wall in the hallway and watched her put clothes into the suitcase on the bed. She had changed into a cream-colored sweater and boot-cut jeans that clung to her ass the way he'd like to. Her low-heeled boots put her at just the right height for him to easily reach that curvy backside if he were to wrap his arms around her. He wondered again what he had gotten himself into. The hair on his arms was standing on end from the energy zinging between them and he doubted he could ever get used to it. Would Murray House, as large as it was, be big enough to escape her? He dragged his gaze away from temptation and focused it on the floor instead.

Eager for a distraction, he caught a glimpse of something peeking out from under the bed. Jayne breezed past him to the living room, her scent wrapped around him, light and floral. He heard her rustling around in the kitchen and glanced back to the bed, curiosity drawing him. Kneeling, he grasped the corner and drew the object out from its hiding place. It was a painting, an unframed canvas. He blew the light layer of dust from the surface, making his sensitive nose twitch, and studied the picture. A high-quality watercolor of the coastline of the town. It looked as though it might have been painted from the cliff road he had driven along coming here. A sense of light radiated from it, making the scene glow. He knew it would have caught his eye hanging in any gallery. He looked to the bottom corner and was stunned to see the signature J Davis. *Jayne painted this?* Why would it be hidden under a bed instead of displayed? The only artwork he had seen on the walls of her apartment were modern prints.

Confused he bent to check under the bed again but there were no more paintings just a large, flat, dusty wooden box. When opened it revealed an array of sealed paint and brushes and other painting and drawing necessities. It had never entered his head that she might be an artist. What would it be like to see all her passion and energy directed at her art? Would she paint for him? Impulsively he closed the box, brushed the dust off and opened Jayne's suitcase. He slid the box into the bottom under the neatly folded clothes just as he heard her footsteps approach. By the time Jayne entered the room he was standing by the window and the suitcase was closed again.

"Ready to go?"

She looked at him, brows lowered in suspicion. "Sure." He avoided her eyes, picked up the suitcase and followed her out of the apartment. He should just ask her about the painting but something told him she wouldn't welcome it. There had to be a very good reason why someone so talented had abandoned her work. With that in mind, how was she going to react when she discovered his addition to her suitcase? Cameron winced internally and resolved to be far, far away when she unpacked.

Chapter Four

ಏ

Jayne shifted in the seat of the hunter-green, four-wheel drive and studied the man beside her. Those magnificent amber-colored eyes of his were hidden behind the sunglasses he had donned as soon as they had gotten into the car, shielding his eyes from the winter sun which sat low in the sky and glittered off the wet road surface with eye-watering intensity. He had told her only that it would take about three hours to get to Murray House. Then he had clammed up and had remained stubbornly silent, refusing to be drawn into conversation. Jayne had been left to study the passing scenery. It was a while before she had noticed that the man beside her was paying just as much attention to their surroundings. The realization that he was checking to see if they were being followed had once again reinforced how serious he was about the threat to her.

They had left the motorway behind about forty minutes ago and joined a narrow country road that wound its way into the hills. Patchy snow and slush had given way to a layer of white crystals over the fields surrounding them. The road was wet and slippery in places, forcing Cam to slow down or risk skidding off the road. Her whole body tensed every time they rounded one of the sharp bends in the road. After the deaths of Megan's and her own parents, she had never really been comfortable in cars. He handled the large vehicle with a confidence that she admired, but it didn't make her feel any better.

Cameron looked relaxed but a sudden tension in his shoulders caused her to glance at the road ahead of them. A temporary sign stood just by the road side and a bit farther on, a policeman stood at the entrance to a small parking place. A vehicle checkpoint. The police often set them up on these small roads where it was easier to control the traffic. They were looking for cars without the right documents and checking that they were roadworthy. Jayne sighed, this car was brand new and there was no way this man would be trying to dodge paying his road tax. Why should he? He could afford it. It still meant at least a twenty-minute delay while they checked it out though.

They were directed into a space behind a white transit van and he opened the window to talk to the officer who had waved them off the road. There was another uniformed officer kneeling by the front tire of the van. In front, there were a couple of cars and a white mobile office with police markings. A set of metal steps led up to a door in the back and Jayne could see a corkboard with papers pinned on it through the grille window. Her attention was drawn back to the man who was now looking at the van's rear tire. Something about him bothered her but she couldn't quite put her finger on it. Vaguely she was aware of Cameron gathering the vehicle documents from the glove compartment and opening the door. He had just gotten out of the car when it clicked.

Trainers.

He was wearing black sneakers.

What policeman wore sneakers when in uniform?

She turned to tell Cameron and saw him scuffling with the policeman. The man was leaning against the door, trapping him and restricting his ability to fight back. She scrambled over the gearshift to help as Cam gave a guttural grunt and cursed viciously. The man with the trainers was coming to his feet and she suspected it was only a matter of time before others followed him. The door flew open as she threw her weight against it. Caught off guard the man stumbled backwards and fell onto the gravel surface. Only her grasp of the steering wheel prevented Jayne from falling out after him. Hastily, she climbed back to her seat as Cameron jumped in behind her.

The well-tuned engine roared to life and he floored the accelerator. The car bounded forward, throwing her off balance, her head hit the door with a resounding thump and she bit her tongue. She found herself sprawling on the floor in front of the passenger seat, the coppery taste of blood filling her mouth. Tires squealed on concrete as Cameron drove them recklessly around corners. She braced herself, suddenly glad she couldn't see where they were going.

"Are they following us?" she asked. He had lost his sunglasses in the struggle and the expression in his amber eyes was fierce. He glanced in the rearview mirror and the car slowed a little.

"Disnae look like it." He reached out and grasped her hand, hauling her back into her seat. Jayne groaned and rubbed the lump that was forming on her head as a number of other sore places began to make themselves known. She pushed them out of her mind and snapped her seat belt into place. "What the hell just happened? That wasn't a real checkpoint, was it?"

He scowled at the road and growled, "No. It wasnae." He scrubbed a hand over his face.

She let the implications of that sink in. She was no fool, it didn't take long. "They were waiting for us. You know what that tells me? They knew *you*. Not me. I would have had no reason to be on this road. Maybe I wouldn't have been in any danger if you hadn't brought me to it."

He didn't seem to hear her. Frowning, he shook his head abruptly like a dog shaking off water then said abruptly, "Can you drive, lass?"

"What? No." She had failed her driving test when she took it a couple of years ago and never got around to taking it again. Okay that wasn't entirely true, actually she had been too much of a coward to take it again. It had been a miracle that Megan had been able to talk her into it the first time.

He shook his head again. "Shit." This time when he looked at her she noticed that his pupils were dilated, the irises just a ring of gold around them. "Bastard stuck a syringe into my side. Must have been a tranquilizer." The car swerved over the white line and he snapped his attention back to the road. But instead of pulling over, he accelerated.

"What the hell are you doing? Didn't you just say they drugged you!? Slow down!"

"No. They could be right behind us. We have to get back to the estate. It's not far, it'll be safe there." His shoulders had begun to droop and he straightened again. "Open the windows, lass."

She did as he asked, pressing the button on the console with fingers that trembled until the electric windows slid down and freezing air blasted over them both. They rounded another corner at a speed that made her dig her nails into the leather seat. The car drifted so near to the hedgerow beside the road that the wing mirror actually brushed along it and her heart flew into her throat, fluttering like a moth caught in a jar. If there had been a ditch beside the road they'd have been in it. Nausea burned in her stomach. She turned back to Cameron, his eyes were beginning to drift shut and he was visibly straining to resist it. A pine forest loomed over them on one side of the road, its sharp earthy scent sweeping through the window. "Tell me we're nearly there, please," she yelled over the noise of the wind.

He nodded, as though it would be too much effort to speak. The car swerved again, the wheels losing purchase on the slippery road for a few seconds. "Cameron!" He jerked his head up and wrestled the car back into the lane. Finally he began to slow down and Jayne sent a silent prayer of thanks to the heavens as they turned onto an unmarked gravel road leading into the trees. Thankfully, the branches seemed to have sheltered it from the worst of the snow, but it was poorly maintained and liberally sprinkled with deep, muddy puddles. They had barely driven a dozen feet down it when they hit one of the potholes, the car lurched to a drunken stop and the engine stalled. Jayne let out a shuddering sigh of relief and unclenched her aching fingers from the leather upholstery. She looked over to find Cameron slumped over in his seat, breathing deep and even.

"My god, you are nuts!"

She leaned across and grabbed the heavy muscles at the top of his arm, digging in her short nails and shaking him. "Cameron! Cam, wake up!" She slapped his face hard enough to leave a faint red handprint. "Come on, wake up!" Nothing, no response. He was out cold. "Shit! Shit! Shit!"

The light was fading and the surrounding woods made it even gloomier, it was already very dark under the trees on either side. Dark enough that she could only see a half a dozen feet into them before the light disappeared into black. Worse, as the winter sun set, the temperature was dropping. It had been warm in the car and they had both left their jackets on the backseat. Shivering, she rolled up the windows and turned the heat back up. Thankfully it was only a stalled engine and the electrical systems were still working. She winced at the thought and superstitiously touched her fingers to the wood paneling on the dashboard, unwilling to tempt the fates. They couldn't stay here all night, even with the heater switched on, not when they could be followed at any time. It was obvious that whoever set up the checkpoint had at least an idea where Cameron lived. She could walk, but there was no way to tell how far along the road she'd have to go before reaching Murray House. No. She'd have to drive, or try to. She looked at the big man in the driver's seat. How on earth was she going to get him out of there and over here? He was a dead weight, there was just no way.

"And this started off as such a nice day," she muttered.

After much tugging and hauling and some grunting she was glad Cameron hadn't been awake to hear, she had the seat back lowered and the seat pushed away from the wheel. Then she had moved him back far enough so that she could sit on the edge of the seat between his legs. The heat of his body radiated through her lower back, distracting her as she studied the dashboard and tried to remember her long-ago driving lessons.

"All right, Jayne, first things first. We need lights… Aha!" She found the switch and turned it on, the powerful headlights flooded the road ahead with light and deepened the shadows. She shivered a little and, feeling a little ridiculous, hit the door locks.

"Okay…engine." She turned the key in the ignition and the engine roared briefly as the car lurched forward then stalled again. "Oops. Neutral, Jayne, neutral." She moved the gearstick and tried again, grinning when the engine started with a well-mannered purr. "Check it out, Cameron, we have liftoff." Soft snoring was her only reply and her grin widened. The quiet sound made him seem more approachable.

"Now if we can only get this very expensive tank moving forward."

It took her a few attempts and a couple more stalls to get the four-wheel drive creeping forward in a low gear. But it was moving, albeit slowly, and Jayne was inordinately pleased with her achievement. Maybe it was time to take up those driving lessons again after all.

It seemed like an eternity before she reached the end of the road in front of a pair of enormous iron gates set into a wall. Her shoulders were tight with the strain of keeping the vehicle moving. Every time it had hit one of the holes in the road, her feet had almost slipped off the clutch and that, in turn, had jolted the car forward. She was surprised not to see a little sweaty smudge on the windshield where her nose had been pressed as she tried to watch for potholes. Beyond the gates, she could see lights in the window of a mansion but she could only hope it was the right one. She might have recognized Cameron's home from Megan's enthusiastic descriptions but it was too dark now to see any details. There was an intercom mounted on a post beside her door and she rolled down the window and pressed the button. Within a few minutes it crackled to life and a woman's voice asked, "Yes?"

"Is this Murray House?"

"Yes it is. What are you doing in Mr. Murray's car?" Suspicion filled the woman's voice.

"My name is Jayne Davis. I'm a friend of Megan and Jack Douglass. I have Cameron—Mr. Murray—here with me, he's been drugged and he's asleep. Can you open the gate?"

"Put on the overhead light." Jayne did as she was asked, lifting the sun visor so that there was no obstruction for the wall-mounted camera.

"Come in, just drive right up to the door."

With a buzz and a click the gates swung open and Jayne drove through, following the concrete driveway beyond. Someone had salted it, leaving a cleared path through the snow up to the huge, sandstone house. She jerked to a stop a few feet from the stone steps and turned the engine off with a sigh of relief. Warm light shone out of the open door and spilled over the woman who waited there. She looked to be in her early fifties. Concern marred the fine features of her face as she rushed down the stairs to the vehicle. Her hair fell in a sleek mahogany bob and she wore black slacks and pastel blue sweater.

It was obvious that Cameron was important to her and Jayne climbed out and stepped back to let her see him. The older woman leaned in the open door to check his pulse and lay a gentle hand against his beard-roughened cheek. Jayne frowned as a pang of what felt very much like jealousy swept through her. Not a romantic jealousy. She somehow knew that Cameron wouldn't have kissed her if he was involved with someone else. More because this woman touched him with such familiarity. Jayne wanted to claim the same right as her own but he wasn't hers.

Apparently satisfied with the condition of the slumbering man, she straightened and offered her hand.

"I'm Mary, Mary MacFarlane, Mr. Murray's housekeeper. Let's get him into the house, then you can tell me what happened."

She eyed the woman doubtfully, she was slender and a good six inches shorter than Jayne herself. How on earth were the two of them going to get him into the house? Mary smiled at her as though reading her mind.

"I'm stronger than I look, love. And I have a secret weapon." She reached into the pocket of her trousers and pulled out a small bottle of old-fashioned smelling salts. "They won't bring him out of it completely, the only thing that will do that is time. If we knew what drug he was given, I could give him an antidote but I don't want to risk it otherwise." Jayne gaped at her and she smiled reassuringly. "Close your mouth, love, you'll catch midgies, I have medical training. Now, come and give me a hand, this might make him alert enough to help us."

Dutifully Jayne did as she was told and got into the passenger side again, kneeling in the seat.

"You might want to sit back just a little bit dear, just in case. These boys do tend to come out of it fighting."

These boys? She did as she was asked, filing her questions away for later as Mary opened the bottle and wafted it under Cameron's nose. The precaution was for nothing though, whatever they had given him still held him in a tight grip. Instead, he woke slowly groaning and struggling to open his eyes. His voice was heavy with sleep as he struggled for awareness.

"Jayne."

"I'm here, we're at the house. We need to get you inside, Cameron, you have to help us."

He focused briefly on her face and something possessive flashed through his eyes before he turned to Mary.

"Mary?"

The housekeeper brushed a hand through his hair. "Yes, it's me. Come on, my love, let's get in the house."

He fell silent and, with their help, pushed himself slowly up until he could get his feet out of the car and stand, leaning heavily on Mary. Jayne scrambled over the seat and tucked herself under his other shoulder so that they could stagger clumsily up the steps and into the house. They passed through a wood-paneled hallway and through a door on the right leading to a living room. "This will have to do." Mary gasped, "There's no way we'll get him upstairs." Cameron's feet were almost dragging now and they had to take more of his weight as the drug pulled him back under. He groaned as they let him fall back onto the cushions of the dark green leather sofa, both of them breathless with exertion. "He can sleep here, I'll get him some blankets and he'll be warm enough with the fire burning."

She leaned over and lowered his shoulders while Jayne lifted his legs so that he was lying flat with his feet hanging over the edge. As they stood he reached out and grasped Mary's wrist, pulling her closer until he could meet her eyes. He said something to her and the woman's startled gaze flew to Jayne and she smiled as though someone had told her she'd won the lottery. Jayne frowned, the muttered words made no sense to her but they obviously meant something to his housekeeper.

What the hell did Derav Kea al *mean?*

Chapter Five

ဆ

Jayne set her suitcase at the foot of the stairs and paused at the living room door. The lights had been dimmed and gentle snoring had resumed from the man on the couch. His face was relaxed in sleep. A plaid blanket covered him, his shoes and socks had been removed and his long bare feet stuck out of the bottom. There was something oddly vulnerable about a man's bare feet, why was that? Shaking her head, she turned away from him and followed the sound of clattering dishes to the back of the house.

She found Mary in a bright, pine kitchen heating something on the stove. It smelled delicious and Jayne drew a deep appreciative breath. In all today's excitement, she had missed lunch and now that it was all over, hunger rolled over her.

"Is stew okay with you, dear? I wasn't sure when Cameron would be back so I made something that could just be warmed."

"It's fine, thank you, what can I do to help?"

"You can set the table and slice some bread, if you don't mind." She nodded toward the counter where she had left two sets of dishes and a fresh loaf. Jayne did as she was asked and it wasn't long before the two women were sitting down to eat.

"Now, why don't you tell me why you brought my boy back to me unconscious?"

Jayne looked up at the woman across from her and tried to gather her thoughts into some kind of order. A rueful smile flitted across her face as she realized it just wasn't going to be possible. This whole day had been like some kind of surreal dream but the bump, throbbing on the back of her head, told her it was real enough.

"I knew that he was going to collect you," Mary prompted. "He thinks you are in danger. I know it has something to do with the person who tried to kill Jack and Megan but he wouldn't tell me what. Stubborn fool."

Jayne smiled at the apt description. She suspected Mary knew more than she was letting on but the housekeeper's face gave nothing away as she recapped the events of the day.

"My goodness, you have had a busy day." She stood and carried the empty plates to the dishwasher.

"That's it? That's all you're going to say?" Jayne asked incredulously.

"What else is there to say? You're here now and both safe, no one can get near the house without us knowing about it." She turned back to Jayne and smiled. "I know it's early yet but you've had a terrible day and you must be tired. Why don't I show you to your room and you can take a warm bath? It'll help to ease those aches and pains." When Jayne looked at her in surprise, she laughed. "I've been a nurse for a long time, love, I know the signs."

Jayne wrinkled her nose, she hadn't realized it was obvious and, truth be told, it wasn't that bad. Apart from a sore head, her neck and shoulders were aching and she knew that her clothing had to conceal some colorful bruises. Nothing terrible, just uncomfortable. She would rather stay here and get some answers to her questions. One look at Mary's face told her that she wasn't going to say any more so she gave in gracefully.

"A bath and some painkillers sound wonderful. Thank you."

She collected her suitcase and followed the housekeeper up to the second floor, feet sinking deeply into the dark, red carpet. Both landings were gallery style and were overlooked by round stained glass windows, which had to be glorious in the sunlight. They depicted a mermaid with a mirror in her right hand and a comb in her left. The stylized writing beneath said *"Tout Prest"* and Jayne wondered briefly if they were a clan crest, which would make sense, given the obvious age of the house. She opened her mouth to ask Mary but the other woman was already climbing the next stairs so she quickened her pace to catch up.

The first floor was unlit but the second glowed with soft light from the glass wall fixtures. It was more modern in décor than she had seen on the first floor with wallpaper in a rich cream rather than the wood paneling. The lighter color softened the red of the carpet. On both sides of the landing, windows looked out of the back of the house along the length of the hall. There were five doors along the opposite wall and another at the end. Mary turned right and stopped at the fourth. "This is yours, it has its own bathroom and you'll find everything you need in there." She nodded toward the doors farther along the corridor. "Cameron's suite is right next to you and the door at the end is his office. I'll see you at breakfast. Goodnight, dear."

Jayne watched the housekeeper's retreating back for a second before opening the bedroom door. She was beginning to have some sympathy for Megan's experience a few months ago. This was just a little bit surreal. She stepped into the room and her mouth dropped open in surprise.

Wow! Megan would love this.

The center of attention was an enormous four-poster bed. It took up most of one wall, its gleaming dark frame draped in what looked like yards of opaque, cream-colored material. The quilt was also cream with little pink flowers embroidered on it and looked as soft and puffy as a cloud. Jayne imagined you could lie down in the middle and never be seen again. The colors were echoed on the walls and the lace curtains at windows. The carpet was pale, pale pink and was so soft, her feet sank a good inch into the pile. She pushed the door closed and stood in the center of the room, suitcase at her feet, afraid to touch anything before she'd washed her hands.

My god, we're not in Kansas anymore.

She lifted her case onto the top of a chest of drawers and opened it, grabbing her nightshirt and toiletry bag from the top. Unpacking it could definitely wait 'til morning. The door opposite the foot of the bed led into a bathroom of white and gold. A large glass shower cubicle was fitted into the corner and a bathtub, large enough to fit three people comfortably, took up most of the rest of the space. Scented candles sat around two sides of it, adding a splash of color. She started filling the tub and rooted in the bathroom cabinet until she found the promised painkillers. She swallowed two and sat on the toilet seat to strip off her clothes while steam filled the room around her.

Amazing. In the space of one afternoon, she had gone from being a grocery store clerk, who had almost stopped living, to this. Car chases and bad guys, an isolated mansion house and a brooding man. There was no doubt about it, Cameron Murray had brought life screaming back into her life in vivid Technicolor.

Things had begun to change the day she had answered Megan's call, but who knows how long she would have procrastinated about it if Cam hadn't shown up on her doorstep. Jayne stood and tested the temperature of the water before turning off the taps. The sudden silence hung in the moist air as she stepped into the tub. She pictured the man downstairs, with his warm, golden skin and the secrets that seemed to hide in his eyes. He was so big. Jayne was tall, so it was unusual to find a man who was so much taller than herself. The kind of man who usually attracted her was also usually slighter in build. *A million years ago, when she was still having sex.*

Cameron was anything but slight with his broad shoulders and muscular chest and arms. *I bet he has a six-pack.* She'd never touched a real six-pack before. He was certainly a temptation that any woman would be hard-pressed to resist, let alone one who hadn't had sex for as long as herself. Judging by the kiss they had shared at the wedding and the incendiary glances he had given her today, that attraction seemed to be returned. However reluctantly. A shiver of anticipation ran through her at the thought, raising goose bumps on her skin. She sank deeper into the warm water and closed her eyes. Cameron Murray had no idea what he was in for.

Hah. Yeah, right, Jayne.

She grinned and shook her head, it was a nice thought. Cameron Murray was a man, in every sense of the word, and the last time she had tried to seduce anyone, he had definitely been a boy when compared to Cameron. Jayne had a feeling she was playing with fire.

* * * * *

The man punched his code into the keypad and waited for the light to flash green. Heavy steel doors slid open with a hiss and he walked into the hallway beyond. The walls were bright white and the reflection from the fluorescent lights stung his night-adjusted eyes. His boots squeaked on the gray vinyl flooring, he winced and shrugged his shoulders uncomfortably. He wished he had been able to change out of the damn uniform before he had answered the summons. He hadn't dared though. He had delayed his report long enough while he had watched the house in the hope he would be able to salvage the operation. He was no coward, had served and fought for his country with pride. Until his commanding officer had caught wind of his retirement scheme. It's not like anyone would have missed those guns anyway. Better than leaving them lying to rust where some kid might pick one up and shoot his mate with it. The way he saw it, he was doing a public service. Still, his knees shook as he knocked on the door to the office.

"Come."

The office was softly lit by a brass lamp on the desk and the vinyl flooring gave way to thick carpeting. A coat stand in one corner held a dark gray suit jacket and a white lab coat. The other corner held a single, locked filing cabinet. A slim laptop, closed at the moment, and two security monitors filled a table against the far wall. One screen was flickering through the various surveillance cameras around the building. The other showed a split-screen of the holding facility where several of the inhabitants paced behind the glass walls. Some were human, some were…not.

The man who sat behind the heavy, wooden desk looked up as he entered. He was fiftyish and still fit, with broad shoulders and a trim waist and dark hair just beginning to be threaded with silver. His shirt was a pristine white and his tie was precisely knotted. He placed the papers he had been reading on top of the pile in front of him, squaring the edges up neatly with his fingertips. When he spoke, his voice was pleasant, friendly even, but his blue eyes were icy.

"Henry. Explain to me why I am sitting here reading papers instead of in the lab with a new subject."

"He wasn't alone, Professor."

"I see." He steepled his neatly manicured fingers and studied him over them. "And did your surveillance not indicate that he was a largely solitary creature?"

"Yes, sir. However, his routine seems to have changed since Dr. York targeted his friend."

The professor lowered his hands to the desk where he drummed his fingers on the table. "Then you're saying the failure of the capture was my fault."

"No! No, sir!" Cold sweat dampened Henry's forehead and trickled down his spine. His stomach roiled greasily. "Dr. York's contributions to the project were invaluable."

"Very true, though his lack of caution in his hunting methods was lamentable. I hate to waste resources but…he was a necessary sacrifice. I do believe he was quite mad toward the end."

The fingers on the table stilled and Henry took a shaky breath as he continued his explanation. "Murray had Jayne Davis in the car with him. She helped him escape."

"Now there's an interesting twist of fate. Two marked females who are close friends. Coincidence or some kind of biological attraction? It might be interesting to study." The professor's eyes narrowed. "Why didn't you catch them?"

"They made it to Murray House, it has extensive security and we weren't equipped to take them there."

"Careless."

That one word was enough to turn Henry's knees to water again. The professor's eyes narrowed. "Has he changed yet?"

"I don't believe so, sir. We still have him under close surveillance."

"It's only a matter of time before he takes her, if he hasn't already." He paused. "I hate breaking in a new employee, but I have no use for a head of acquisitions who can't acquire. One last chance, Henry, make sure you are properly prepared this time. I suggest you and your men move quickly. He's of less use to me if they bond."

* * * * *

Cameron groaned as consciousness stole over him. His head pounded in time with his heartbeat and his neck and back ached. *Did someone get the license plate of the truck that ran over me?* He shifted, trying to find a more comfortable position and nearly fell off the bed. His eyes flew open in surprise and he found himself stretched out on his leather sofa. *What the hell am I doing in the living room?* Memories of the previous night flooded back, from the punch of the needle in his side, to the suffocating effects of the drug as he fought it in a frantic race to reach his estate. He didn't remember reaching the house, his memories became fuzzy as they approached the access road, then nothing.

Jayne. Was she safe? No sooner had he thought it, he registered the faint prickle of magic on his skin that signified her presence. Relieved, he closed his eyes again and concentrated his senses on the house around him. He detected her scent mingling with the comforting smells of home and it felt…right. Beneath the ticking of the grandfather clock and the familiar household sounds, he could hear her laughing with Mary in the kitchen at the back of the house. *How did they get to the house?* He knew she couldn't drive, *could he have driven the final part of the journey and not remembered?* Unless she had walked. It was a mile of gravel road through a forest, in darkness. He knew enough about her to know that she wouldn't hesitate if she felt it was the only option. Anger filled him at the thought of her having to put herself at risk like that. Anger at the men who had ambushed them and anger at himself for letting it happen.

Had they used the same ruse with Nick? It was clearly well equipped and practiced. Did Nick have time to be angry at himself for falling for it? The drug they used was powerful and thanks to Jayne's intervention, he suspected he hadn't received the full dose. Nick had been alone and outnumbered and that was his fault. Cameron wouldn't rest until he found the men responsible and made them pay. It was the least he could do for a man who had been like a brother to him.

Wearily, he rolled to his feet and stretched out the kinks the sofa had folded into his long body. He scrubbed a hand over his chin and found that the stubble was fast on the way to becoming a beard. Jayne's laughter rang out again and he turned toward it, letting her warmth wash over his skin. He should go upstairs and try to put some distance between them but her voice drew him like a siren's song. He found himself following it until he stood unnoticed in the kitchen doorway surrounded by the energy of the *Ceangal*. The two women were at the sink with their backs toward him, chatting as they washed and dried the delicate china. Their topic of conversation seemed to be movie stars and Cam didn't know whether to be relieved or irritated that they weren't talking about him. Or worried that the subject had come and gone and he'd never know what had been said.

Mary had worked for his family for twenty-five of his thirty-three years and had been his only family since he was sixteen. She knew everything about him, it wouldn't take her long to see the connection between himself and Jayne. She disagreed, intensely, with his decision not to take a mate and would see this as an opportunity to change his mind.

Jayne turned toward him as he stepped into the room and, for endless minutes, he found himself unable to look away. The sound of a throat being cleared jolted him and he scowled and headed for the coffeepot. More shaken than he cared to admit, he kept his back to the women and concentrated on pouring himself some coffee.

Mary broke the silence first, her voice soft with concern. "Are you all right, Cameron, dear? I checked on you in the night and you seemed to be in a more natural sleep so I thought it best to leave you alone."

He fought the urge to squirm like a teenager in the face of her easy affection in front of Jayne and shrugged. "I'm fine. Just a bit of a headache, that's all."

He could feel Jayne's relief and curiosity and did his best to ignore both as he turned back to face them. Mary took a step toward him but stopped when he glowered at her. He knew she wouldn't be satisfied until she had poked and prodded at him but he'd be damned if he would let her do it here. He studied his houseguest through narrowed eyes, satisfied that she seemed to be uninjured. She looked well rested. Her hair was pulled back into a high ponytail and her creamy complexion was clear of shadows. He suspected that her lilac sweater and jeans might cover some bruising but she seemed to be unaffected by it.

"How did we get to the house?"

"I drove us."

A blush crept over her face as he watched and an image flashed through his mind of Jayne sitting between his legs in the front seat of his four-wheel drive. Irritated with his body's response to the provocative memory, he glared at her.

"I thought you said you couldnae drive?"

She frowned at him. "I can't. I have, however, had some lessons, they were enough to get the car moving and get us here. Mary helped me get you into the house. You should be thanking me, not snarling at me." She swept out of the room before he could answer and he growled in frustration. Movement caught his eye and he turned see Mary smiling at him. He held up his hand to silence her. "Dinnae say a word, dinnae even think it. It's not goin' tae happen."

The smile was gone but her eyes twinkled. "Okay."

"Ah mean it."

"Fine."

Cam shook his head and walked away from her. He had work to do, maybe now that he knew Jayne was safe, he would be able to get on with it. He was on the stairs when Mary's triumphant whisper reached his sensitive ears.

"Yes!"

When he stepped from his shower twenty minutes later, his mood was worse, rather than better. The coffee sat untouched on the bedside table where he had left it when his stomach had revolted at his first sip. His head was still pounding with the lingering effects of the tranquilizer, despite the pain reliever he had taken. He swiped a towel over his body in quick, angry strokes. A cold shower had done nothing to dampen his lust. A condition intensified by the fact that his housekeeper—*ex*-housekeeper—had put Jayne in the bedroom next door. He could feel her there.

She was unpacking. Relaxed and faintly excited, looking forward to exploring the house and grounds. Their connection wasn't strong enough yet for him to catch more than the occasional thought or emotion, especially when his guard was up. But that didn't prevent the flow of magic between them. It washed over him like waves over sand, wearing away his resistance. Taking a piece of his control with it every time it ebbed away. Cursing, he threw his towel into the laundry basket and dressed with quick efficiency in worn jeans and a sweatshirt. As he tied his damp hair back with a strip of leather, he felt a jolt of annoyance from Jayne. Abruptly, he remembered his addition to her luggage and cringed.

Endless moments passed before the expected knock on his door came.

"Come in."

He braced himself but the woman who entered the room didn't look angry. Instead she looked…happy. He frowned at her, confused by the mixture of happiness and sorrow she was broadcasting. She was close enough to touch and he balled his fists to prevent himself from doing just that. Her smile faded and she cleared her throat as though she too felt the building tension.

"Why did you put the paint box in my bag?"

"I don't know, it was an impulse. I saw it under the bed and…" He shrugged his shoulders and shook his head, watching her warily. "You're very talented, I wanted to see you paint."

"Thank you, maybe you will." She laughed softly. "Cameron, you can stop looking at me like I'm an unexploded bomb. I'm not angry." She took a step closer and laid her hand on his arm and he felt the contact go through him like electricity. "Oh, I was annoyed at first. I haven't painted in a long time. It was a part of me I put aside for reasons I'm not even sure of anymore. But things are different now, *I'm* different now. I suppose you are partly responsible for that, so thanks."

She leaned forward and placed her lips on his. He froze, muscles trembling against instinct. He closed his eyes and felt the softness of her mouth and was surrounded by the light, vaguely floral scent of her perfume. It overlaid the unique scent that was Jayne, a scent he couldn't have described if there was a gun to his head. A scent he knew he would recognize anywhere. His heartbeat pounded in his ears as it pumped the heady rush of his excitement through his body.

And then she was gone.

He opened his eyes and watched her walk out the door, aching to follow her.

Chapter Six

℘

Fat snowflakes swirled and drifted down onto the wide lawn and coated the pine trees like icing sugar. Jayne sat in the cozy warmth of the kitchen conservatory and watched them fall from a sky heavy with clouds. As they had been falling more or less nonstop since the first morning she woke here. If it didn't stop soon, she was going to have to brave the elements and go outside anyway. She was starting to get a bit stir-crazy. The house felt empty though she knew it wasn't. Mary was in her private quarters at the far end of the building and she knew that the housekeeper would join her if she asked. She wasn't going to ask though, because the woman deserved a little time to herself. She had been entertaining Jayne for the last two days.

They had spent part of the first day exploring Murray House. Cam had inherited it when his parents had died. Mary had reluctantly told her that his mother had died when he was fifteen and his father when he was sixteen. There had been both sadness and anger in her face and she wouldn't say any more. Jayne didn't press, she knew from personal experience that it was a sensitive subject. After that, Mary had avoided most questions about Cam, focusing instead on the history of the house.

It was enormous. Jayne had counted sixteen bedrooms on the first and second floors with rooms on the opposite side of the hallways set up as separate sitting rooms. She could see now that the kitchen was an addition to the back of the house. The original had been tucked away in the basement where there was now a bright fully equipped gym. Very fully equipped. The housekeeper had showed her a secure room behind the mirrors, complete with a computer connected to the house security system, a phone, weapons, a cot and enough food and water for a week. The fact that Cameron felt the need to have one spoke volumes about his life.

Mary had a suite on the ground floor in the left wing. The rest of the rooms down there were entertainment and living areas, including a large library that made her green with envy. The house was decorated in a strangely appealing mixture of modern, Victorian and Georgian styles. Even Jayne's untrained eye picked out a multitude of antiques throughout. Here and there, the mermaid clan crest was repeated on fireplaces, furniture, china and other, smaller things. The motto "*Tout Prest*" she had discovered meant "Always Ready" and from what she had seen so far, it was one the current laird lived up to.

It was clear that Cameron Murray was a very wealthy man, indeed. And a private one if the absence of staff was any indication. Didn't he ever get bored? Jayne wasn't exactly a social butterfly anymore but this much solitude would give her the screaming meemies in a very short time. She hoped, fervently, that they didn't get snowed in.

The man of the house was in his office where he had spent most of his time since their conversation in the kitchen. He had better be working on finding out who the fake policemen were 'cause she couldn't stay here indefinitely. She suspected he was avoiding her. Lunchtime had come and gone and he hadn't come down to eat. He had missed breakfast too. In fact, she hadn't seen him at any of the mealtimes. She suppressed a twinge of worry, but he was a big boy, perfectly capable of looking after himself. He probably had a minibar complete with refrigerator and snacks up there. If he wanted to creep around and eat alone, who was she to argue?

He *was* lonely.

She knew it with a deep down certainty. She didn't question the knowledge, she just felt it. The more time she spent near him, the more she felt she knew him. Somehow her feelings had slipped past lust and into something far less easy to define. Which was ridiculous, because they had hardly spent ten minutes in each other's company since they arrived.

She had only caught brief glimpses of him as he went to and from his bedroom. There had been one particularly charged encounter on the stairs when he had been returning from the gym. He had been dressed in shorts and a T-shirt which clung to his broad chest and had a towel around his neck. His burnished hair was slicked back into a ponytail. It had obviously been a pretty intense workout, sweat had dampened the hair at his temples and the front of his shirt. She caught the clean, sharp smell of it and felt the heat radiate from his body as he stood on the step below her. For endless moments, he had stared at her with an almost predatory stillness. His nostrils flared and his chest expanded as he drew in a breath and shuddered. A battle seemed to be fought and won within his eyes and he had slipped silently past her and on up the stairs. Jayne had been left breathless and he hadn't even touched her.

Mary talked about him very little, but when she did, it was with visible affection. As a child, he had apparently been a prankster. Playing tricks on the members of the household with annoying regularity. He had done things to and around priceless antiques which had made Jayne's blood run cold.

Now, Jayne saw a man who loved his family and friends but rarely showed it. She still thought he could be rude...and arrogant, though. Had it only been his parents' deaths that had changed him? Why was he going to such trouble to isolate himself? Every time she saw him, she saw a longing and desire in his eyes that made her want to go to him. Take him into her body and heart and keep him there. She sighed. Megan was right, she read far too many romances. Still, there was no denying the feelings. Hadn't Megan told her the very same thing about how she felt about Jack? Megan had told her a lot before she decided to get all cryptic.

The hell with suspected. She *knew* Cameron was avoiding her. She also knew there were things he was keeping from her.

Why exactly she was here, for instance, he had been a little too vague about that. So was Mary and let's not forget Megan and Jack. They were all definitely hiding something. Dammit, why did everyone seem to be keeping secrets from her lately? It was beginning to get annoying. She was no fool and as impossible as it may seem she had a good idea what Jack's secret was but was it Cam's too? She thought about his big, muscular body, his—catlike?—grace of movement and the air of danger that surrounded him. That golden mane and the intensity of his amber gaze… She laughed. Or she could just be letting her imagination run away with her.

Jayne glanced back toward the hallway and smiled. She could always just ask him. "So…Cameron, do you spend part of your time as a cat?" That would certainly get a response from him. What's the worst that could happen? He wouldn't throw her out. For reasons known only to himself, he evidently felt responsible for her and felt she was in danger. He couldn't really avoid her more and still keep an eye on her. Or—if she really let her imagination take over—he might say yes and suddenly start sprouting fangs and claws and fur.

Cool.

Boredom and curiosity are wonderful and terrifying things. With a grin, she rose from the table, left the snowy scene behind her and headed for Cam's office before she could change her mind.

By the time she reached his closed door some of her boldness had seeped away but she gathered it back, knocked and walked into the large room. The curtains were open at the windows in front of her and the ones on either side, letting in the cold, gray light. A computer sat on a large curved desk in the middle of the floor. Cameron sat behind it, brows drawn down in a frown, as usual, while he toyed with a pen on the desktop. An empty glass sat beside him with traces of what looked like milk in it and beside that was a mug with black coffee gently steaming.

"Don't you ever smile?" she blurted.

"Hardly ever. What do you want?"

She looked around, stalling for time, searching for the courage that had once again deserted her.

"Nice office."

The walls were pale in color and the floor looked like polished oak. She had been right about the minibar. It stood against the left-hand wall. Two chairs and a small sofa in black leather were grouped in front of it around a glass-topped table. The right side of the room was taken up by more desk space, shelves and various storage units. Every surface was taken up by every conceivable office machine and gadget. It was clear that this was very much a workspace and the organized clutter all around told her it was used often. Cam watched her in silence, waiting in that unnerving way of his. *So, how do we go about this? Do I just blurt it out or do I try to ease my way into it? Right. How exactly do you ease into that particular subject? "Shame about the weather, oh and by the way…?"* She snorted and Cam raised one eyebrow in query.

"Jayne? Was there something you wanted to ask me?"

"Yes. Yes, there is. I've been spending a lot of time the last couple of days on my own and, well, it's given me time to think. I've been thinking about a conversation that Megan and I had a few months ago and I just wondered…" She walked up to the desk and leaned her hands on the polished surface, watching his face carefully.

"Are you a shapeshifter?"

The pen dropped from his fingers and he placed his hand over it, stilling its movement. Shock followed by anger flickered briefly over his handsome features before he quickly schooled them back into their usual impassive lines.

"What the hell are you talkin' about? Are you off your bloody head, woman?"

"Nope. At least I don't think so. So what about it, Cam, is that what you're hiding from me?" She walked around the table to stand in front of him and noted the white-knuckled fist resting in his lap.

"Dinnae be daft, there's no such thing. Who's been fillin' your head with this nonsense—Mary?"

"Now that's interesting. That you should think it was Mary, I mean. I wonder what she would tell me if I asked her the same question."

His gaze stayed steady on hers and there was suddenly a heat there that had nothing to do with anger. "She likes legends and fairytales and she'd tell you the same."

"You're probably right. She loves you and isn't likely to reveal any of your secrets. Just so you know though, I'm not convinced."

He reached for her hand and drew her into the vee of his legs.

"Well then, I guess I'll just have to do my best to convince you I'm all man, won't I?"

Jayne laughed. "That was a very bad line." Cam grasped her hips and rubbed his cheek against her stomach. She shivered and combed her fingers through his unbound hair. "But effective." His hands tightened on her briefly and a shudder ran through his big frame. He pulled her down onto his lap and buried his face in the curve of her neck. He drew in a deep breath as though savoring the scent of her skin and moaned. A fine tremor shook his body and she wrapped her arms around him. She felt the hard ridge of his arousal, the heat burning her even through the worn fabric of their jeans. Again he rubbed his cheek against her, like a cat marking its territory. He whispered, "*Oh, god.*"

She urged his face up to hers and took his lips in a kiss that shook him with its intimacy. Jayne poured everything she felt into the kiss. She couldn't get close enough. She wanted to climb inside him, wanted him inside her. Her skin felt sensitized, alive. Desperate for the touch of his hands. But he had fisted them in the fabric of her sweater so that the only naked contact between them was her mouth on his as their tongues mated. He tasted like coffee and smelled like the outdoors. Like the earth and the pine trees in the woods outside the windows. He pulled away enough that his words brushed hot against her lips. "Ah shouldnae be doing this."

Jayne nipped at his jaw. "Yes, you should."

"We..." He took her lips again and she found she was trembling almost as much as he was. "We need to stop." He almost growled the words.

"Don't you dare."

"It's almost too late. Ah have to, before Ah have nae choice." He pulled away, breathless and lifted her to her feet in one motion. "Ah cannae do this. Ah'm sorry, lass. God, you have nae idea how sorry."

"I can't believe you're doing this again. I know you want me as much as I want you. What's going on, Cameron?"

He shook his head and plowed a hand through his hair. "Ah cannae explain. Please... Please just go. Stay away from me. For both our sakes."

Jayne stood her ground on shaky legs and tried to pull her scattered wits back together. "You can't say something like that and not give me some kind of explanation." She stared at him, barely resisting stamping her feet in frustration as it became obvious that he wasn't going to say any more. An electronic chime rang from the computer behind him and a cheerful voice sang out, *"You've got mail,"* breaking the awkward silence.

"Okay, fine. I'll leave, but you know all you've done is make me more curious." With that parting shot, she turned on her heel and left the room. She needed a shower. A cold one.

* * * * *

"Shit... Fuck... Bloody buggering hell!"

Cam ground the heels of his hands into his eyes and tried to bring his body back under control. If he wasn't very careful, Jayne Davis was going to be his downfall. Even now it was taking almost everything he had not to chase her down and make her his. She was meant to be his.

His *fíor cèile*.

He would *not* take her though. He couldn't risk ending the same way his parents and so many of his kind had.

She knew about them. Not everything, but enough to be dangerous. How the hell had she found out? Megan must have told her or hinted enough that she had put two and two together. It was the only explanation. Jayne hadn't believed anything he had told her to the contrary. All he could do was continue to deny it. After all, what she believed and what she could prove were entirely different things. He knew he could trust her not to talk to anyone else about it. If not for his sake, then for the sake of her friend and her new husband. That would have to be enough.

He turned back to the computer and the e-mail that had provided such a timely interruption. It had been sent through his company address and had no subject. He didn't recognize the sender except to note that the address indicated it came from a public library account. Curious, he opened it.

Have you lost a cat?

His name is Nick.

If this cat is yours, please respond with a description and I will be in touch with his location.

It had to be a joke. But then surely no one who knew Nick Douglass was a shifter would dare. Cam read the note again not quite able to believe his eyes. Slowly anger replaced the disbelief. It didn't take long to find that the account holder was John Doe and that it had indeed come from a library in the city of Glasgow. He had no doubt that the sender was long gone.

There was little chance he would find them since they would have been able to access the account from any one of many libraries in the city.

It could be a fishing expedition, bait for a trap. After all, it seemed that the people responsible for the disappearance of shapeshifters were aware of him. Jayne had been right when she said it was likely him they were trying for with their roadside trap. This may just be an attempt to draw him away from the safety of Murray House to a place where he could be captured. The only way to find out for sure was to play along. His reply was as carefully worded as the original e-mail. Stating that his cat Nick had black hair and blue eyes and had been believed to have been killed and that he was eager for his safe return.

Cam thought briefly of getting in touch with Jack and decided to wait until he knew whether the e-mail was a genuine lead. He knew Jack would be back in a heartbeat if he thought they might have a clue to his brother's whereabouts. One thing was certain, Cameron wanted to be ready for any outcome and the best way to do that was to call in the security team. He just hoped the outcome wasn't going to confirm his worst fears and lead to the discovery of his friend's body.

Contacting the team had been easy. A quick phone call was all it took to ensure their arrival at the house later that evening. Mary would be pleased to see them and Cameron himself was looking forward to spending some time with his friends. Although it would no doubt lead to more arguments about why he could no longer be an active member. Only Chris really understood his reasoning and even he didn't agree fully.

He missed them.

Until a little more than two years ago, Cam had been an integral part of the team. His skill with computers and security systems had been invaluable. Then he had begun to show signs of entering his mating cycle. At first, it hadn't been too bad, he had been sure his willpower was strong enough to resist the compulsion to take a mate. But as his cycle progressed, it became a huge problem.

His appetite had declined. Insomnia plagued him and he started to become distracted and short-tempered. His libido increased and his cock was hard more often than not. He found himself being aggressive and combative with other males with little provocation. Once or twice, their work had brought them into contact with marked, unmated females. Cameron had been next to useless as he found he had to concentrate all his efforts on fighting his instincts. It made him a liability, causing unnecessary risk to himself and the other team members. Since he had sworn against ever taking a mate, he had seen no other option other than to leave the team.

Ultimately, he had ended up retreating to Murray House where he stayed as much as possible in order to try to ride it out. Thanks in a large part to Mary's medical knowledge and his own determination, he had kept the worst of the effects of the cycle at bay. Until Jack Douglass had landed on his doorstep four months ago. That's when his carefully ordered life had started to go straight to hell.

His insomnia was worse than ever and he was exercising himself to exhaustion to try to get some sleep. Mary had threatened him with sleeping pills more than once. His appetite had gone from poor to nonexistent and it was only a matter of time before it became obvious. The high-calorie drinks and meals were only going to help for so long. Then there was the fact that he felt like a walking hormone and the answer to two years of abstinence was sharing his house. A house that definitely wasn't big enough. To top it all off, by this time tomorrow, there were going to be four more men under the same roof. Shapeshifters. A fact that, with his current run of luck, would not get by Jayne for long. Particularly in Christopher's case. Cameron dropped his head in his hands and groaned. For the first time he wondered whether it might just be easier to give in.

To everything.

Chapter Seven

ℬ

Under the pine trees at the edge of the wide lawn, Henry sheltered from the bitter snow. He and another one of his men had hiked over the hill that morning. They had joined the two men he had already in place and set up a small camp at the far side of the loch. They were armed with both tranquilizers and guns in case things got out of hand but Murray would be no use to them dead. All day they had been watching in turns with high-powered binoculars and thermal imaging cameras. Waiting for darkness to fall and the lights to go out. Then it would be safer to approach the house and disable the motion sensors and alarm system. The snow was a problem at the moment, making for poor visibility, but later it would be an advantage.

He didn't think the couple had bonded yet since they had apparently spent most of the last forty-eight hours in opposite ends of the house. There was a small chance that he was wrong though and it scared the hell out of him. There had been a moment earlier that day, when he had watched through the windows as the couple had been hot and heavy in the office chair, that he had thought it was all over. They had stopped though, for whatever reason, and since neither one of them had changed, he figured he was safe.

Not for the first time, he wished he hadn't taken the professor up on his job offer. Prison would have been the better deal after all. There was a much bigger chance of getting out of there with your life. After this job, he was getting out, the professor could find himself a new "head of acquisitions". The money wasn't worth it anymore. At this rate, he wasn't going to be alive to spend it anyway.

He shifted slightly, clenching and unclenching hands that had begun to go numb from the cold. The sound of approaching vehicles broke the silence of the evening. Moments later, a voice murmured from his headset, "Sir, I've got four vehicles on the road approaching the gate."

"Watch them, I want descriptions."

What the hell were they doing getting visitors at this time? Moments passed and he listened intently, heard the car doors slam.

"Looks like four men and a woman. They're inside, sir, no clear ID. Damn snow. They were all covered up. Had luggage though, looks like they're staying."

"I want to know who they are."

"Yes, sir."

Henry cursed silently. It would be stupid to try for the house now. Unless circumstances changed, his best bet was to wait and keep watching for his chance. And if he was too late, then he was just going to have to disappear a little bit sooner than planned.

* * * * *

Jayne was in the library when she heard the cars in the driveway. She had been trying to read for the last couple of hours without great success. Her mind kept wandering back to the scene in Cameron's office earlier. She was still clueless about why he kept pulling away from her. It was getting incredibly frustrating and she'd give almost anything to be able to read his mind. Since that wasn't an option, she was just going to have to work harder at convincing him to open up. Meantime, it was still snowing and boredom was circling her.

Tomorrow she was going outside, snow or not. It was only water after all, she wouldn't melt. Poor Mary had done her best to entertain her again at dinner. Another dinner at which there had been no sign of Cam. Mary had shrugged it off, saying that he didn't keep to strict mealtimes and that he usually preferred to eat alone. But Jayne had seen worry in the woman's eyes and it had made anxiety flutter in her own stomach. Something was definitely going on with that man.

She put down her book and got to the window in time to see five people gathering bags from the trunks of the vehicles. As the first person climbed the front steps, her spirits rose with them. She followed her curiosity down the hallway and heard Mary's excited voice drifted toward her.

"Come in. Come in out of the cold. Oh, Rianne, it's so nice to see you! You don't get home often enough."

"It's great to see you, Mum."

"Where are my boys?"

Jayne reached the doorway and stood in the shadows to watch. Even if she hadn't heard the woman's reply, she would have identified her immediately as Mary's daughter. The resemblance was unmistakable in the high cheekbones and smiling mouth. Her short hair was a lighter brown than her mother's but they shared the same soft gray eyes. The last four newcomers came into the entryway one at a time, dumping their bags in a pile at the bottom of the stairs. The first, a man with black hair and dark eyes lifted Mary off her feet. He spun her in a circle, placed a loud kiss on her cheek and passed her to the auburn-haired, hazel-eyed man behind him who repeated the cycle. The housekeeper laughed and fussed over them affectionately, helping them brush the snow off and taking their coats.

"Ciaran… Jonathon! You're early. Cameron said it would be very late when you got here."

The first man responded in a voice that was thick with Ireland. "Snow made the roads quiet. We made good time."

The auburn-haired man grinned. "If it were up to the puppy here, we would have been a couple of hours later. He drives like an old woman." He was as upper-class English as his friend was Irish.

"Shut up, Tigger! How much good would we have been to Cam if we had slid into a ditch?"

"Jon has a point, I almost rear-ended you guys a couple of times," Rianne interjected.

"That, my darlin', would be the fault of your own self. You were obviously too close."

"Now, wait just a minute, don't you try to turn this around on me!"

Mary smiled, shaking her head at their antics and turned to the next man who entered. He had very short hair which was as white as the snow on his shoulders though there was nothing old about him. He was slighter in build and had three silver earrings in one ear and one through his eyebrow and was dressed in a long black leather duster over leather pants. He scowled at the bickering of other three, his whole demeanor screaming bad attitude. Jayne suspected he could be a very scary man. His eyes were pale, pale blue that only warmed briefly when he greeted Mary with a kiss. "Fynn." He said nothing, only stepped aside to let the last of the four men come inside.

Jayne saw the softening of Mary's expression as she waited for him. He was the largest of the four and all but dwarfed Cam's housekeeper as she pulled him into her arms before he could even take off his hooded coat. "Christopher. It's so good to see you." They embraced in silence for a few moments before he stepped away and began to unzip his coat. He had the front half undone when he suddenly froze and lifted his head, staring right at Jayne.

When he spoke, his voice was a deep bass rumble, his words slightly blurred as though his vocal cords had been damaged in some way. It made the hair all over her body stand up.

"Mary, you have a guest."

There was silence in the hallway. Almost as one, Jayne felt all of their gazes fall on her though she stood in the shadows and knew she hadn't made a sound. She suddenly thought she knew exactly how a gazelle felt when it heard rustling in the grass behind it. Jayne stepped forward into the light, ignoring the part of her that urged her to run and hide.

"Hi. Sorry, I didn't want to intrude."

Mary stepped forward to take her hand and draw her into the group.

"This is Jayne Davis. She's Cameron's guest, I daresay he'll tell you about it later. Jayne, this is my daughter Rianne and her colleagues. They run a security company, Cameron used to work with them. Still does occasionally as a consultant."

Jayne suspected that they handled a lot more than security but she said nothing as Mary introduced them each in turn.

"Ciaran McCord."

Ciaran took her hand and kissed her knuckles, making her smile. "It's right pleased I am to meet you, Jayne."

"Just ignore him dear, he's a rogue. Thinks all he has to do is use that brogue of his and women will fall at his feet."

"He might be right," Jayne said and Ciaran grinned at her. "But then I had an Irish father and so the accent has an entirely different meaning for me."

"Ah, now then, that just makes me want to try and change your mind."

She laughed and he released her hand as Mary moved her along and gestured to the man with the auburn hair and friendly hazel eyes. He introduced himself as Jonathon Pembroke, clasping her hand briefly in his.

"Fynn," the man leaning against the wall with his arms folded nodded briefly at her, his face impassive, "and Jonathon's brother, Christopher Pembroke." Jayne turned to find that the man had taken his jacket off while her back was turned. Her voice froze in her throat as she stared at him. He watched her in silence, as though waiting for her judgment. He was a big man, maybe an inch or two taller than Cameron but it was more than just his size that rendered her speechless.

His hair was the same auburn as his brother's but streaked through with black and gold and white. It was just long enough that it covered his ears and brushed his collar. His eyes were gold edged with light clear green, like a brighter, sharper version of Jonathon's. There was something different about his face that she couldn't quite put her finger on, something almost...feline. She stepped forward and held her hand out for his. After the briefest hesitation he took it.

"Pleased to meet you, Christopher."

He nodded and released her hand. "Chris."

Jayne narrowed her eyes, she could have sworn she caught a glimpse of fangs in his mouth. She waited and was disappointed when he remained silent. Tension had built she hadn't been aware of but was suddenly gone and Ciaran, Jon and Rianne began arguing again about driving skills. Mary deftly broke it up when she grasped her daughter's arm and started toward the kitchen.

"How about some hot chocolate to warm you all up before you go upstairs to your rooms? Christopher, I believe Cameron is in his office, I'm sure you want to talk to him. Why don't I bring some up to you both?"

"No need, Mary. I'll bring him down, make him socialize." The big man nodded and started up the stairs while Mary led the rest into the kitchen, leaving Jayne looking up toward the second floor with suspicion.

"Come on, Jayne, you can help me keep these boys under control."

Sighing, Jayne followed the summons.

The moment he heard the knock on his door Cameron knew who it would be and called out, knowing the other man wouldn't enter without an invitation.

"Come in, Chris."

He rose from the sofa and they grasped hands and drew each other into a back-slapping embrace.

"It's been too long."

"It has. I take it you haven't received any more details about Nick?"

"No. Nothing. I haven't been able to find out anything more about the person who sent the message and it's damned frustrating! All we can do is wait."

"We've waited this long, Cam, I don't think a few more hours is going to make much difference." He felt his friend's sympathy, saw it in his expression, and knew that he too suspected Nick was dead. "In the meantime why don't you tell me what you, of all people, are doing with an unmated, marked female in your house?"

"Going slowly mad." He shook his head and sat. When Chris had joined him, he told him how and why Jayne Davis had come to be there. "Did you bring the stuff I asked you for?"

"Yes, I asked Jon to stop for it." He smiled. "She doesn't strike me as a woman who's afraid of much. You could have called one of us, Cam, we would have watched her for you."

"No. I thought of that, but I couldnae face having another man do it, never mind another shifter. And now she's under my roof and I had to call you anyway. So I'm sitting up here, where I won't be tempted to rip someone's head off for looking at her the wrong way." He met his friend's gaze. "She's my *fìor cèile*."

"I'm sorry, Cam."

He laughed bitterly. "Why? It's no' your fault. We both knew it would happen eventually. I was just kidding myself to think I would be able to avoid it. I'm just not ready, I'll never be ready. What if it's the same?"

"I know it's not what you wanted but…you're not your parents, Cam."

"Ah have them *in* me, Chris, and the *Ceangal* destroyed them both!" Cameron's brogue increased along with his frustration.

"No. They destroyed each other!" Chris' frustration beat at him. "Your mother was weak, she couldn't cope with the demands of the *Ceangal*. She hated your father for what he was and he should never have taken her. It wasn't a true bond, he could have walked away and didn't! That's what caused their deaths, not the mating bond. I know the bond doesn't always have a happy ending, hell, look at me! But despite this," Chris gestured the length of his body, "I'd still risk anything to have again what you have right under your nose. Susan and I didn't have long, but we were happy, Cam."

Chris stood and laid a hand on his shoulder. "For what it's worth, neither Jon nor Fynn have entered their cycle yet and you know you have nothing to worry about from me."

Cameron looked at his friend, seeing the traces of his animal and knowing his jeans and polo-neck sweater concealed more. His voice was still distorted by vocal cords that weren't quite human but they were both grateful for it. It hadn't been so very long since Chris hadn't been able to speak at all. "How are you, Chris, really?"

"Hanging on. It's not going to get any better, Cam, this is as good as it gets and it took three years to get this far. I still have to watch my temper or things can get out of control. At least I can go out in public now, if I'm careful."

"And Becca?"

Affection and humor chased away the lingering sadness briefly. Chris smiled and shrugged. "She's six. She liked it better when her daddy looked more like a kitty cat." His smile faded. "What are you going to do about Jayne?"

"I don't know, Chris. I just don't know anymore."

"Come downstairs, drink some hot chocolate and make Mary happy. I'll try to make sure you don't kill anyone."

Cam stood and made an effort to throw off his fears. "I'm not sure, Chris... Ry, Ciaran and Jon in the same room? I think it'll be a toss-up between me and Fynn as to who snaps first. You think you can handle us both?"

Chris laughed, slapped him on the back and followed him out of the room. "You I'm pretty sure I can take, at least you'll listen to reason, eventually. I might need some help with Fynn though!"

When the two men reached the kitchen, Mary was just pouring the rich hot chocolate into mugs. Cameron felt the energy of the *Ceangal* swirl around him, through him and his gaze immediately sought out Jayne. When he found her sitting at the table with Jon, he had to fight the desire to go over and drag the younger man out of his seat. She liked him, thought he was funny and charming. Cam heard the thoughts go through her head and was suddenly glad for Chris' silent presence behind him. Giving himself time to get a grasp on his instincts, Cam looked around the room.

Beside the stove, Rianne and Ciaran were fighting about the benefits of marshmallows and consuming most of the packet between them. Ciaran and Rianne had been fighting like brother and sister almost from the moment Ciaran had joined the team five years ago. Mary broke up this argument by snatching the marshmallows out of the Irishman's hand. Shaking her head as he pretended to pout.

Rianne had cut her hair shorter since the last time he saw her and he was relieved to see she had let the blue highlights grow out. A slight smile curved his lips as he remembered that it had been he who had freaked out when she had first dyed her hair. It had been fluorescent green that time and he supposed the electric blue had been an improvement. Mary had merely agreed with her daughter that yes, they were eye-catching. She had laughed when Cameron had objected and told him it was only hair. It would have been entirely different if her daughter had dyed *herself* green. The very possibility that

Ry *might* actually do that had worried him every time she went out of the house for weeks.

Cam felt eyes on him and turned to see Fynn leaning against the counter on the opposite side of the room. He watched with cold blue eyes, keeping himself separate from everyone else in the room, as usual. He looked much the same as he always did. Though he now had three earrings in his ear instead of two. It made Cameron wonder what else he had added under his thin black sweater and leather pants. Last time he had seen him, there had been a ring through his nipple and several tattoos on his body. Waste of money if you asked Cam since all the tattoos would vanish after his first shift. The newest piercings too, unless he left them in when he changed. He nodded at the other man and received an acknowledging tilt of Fynn's head in return.

Feeling more in control, he walked in.

Chapter Eight

❧

Conversation stopped and for a moment there was silence before Ciaran and Jon called out greetings. Rianne dashed forward and jumped into his arms. "Cameron!"

He kissed her cheek and set her on her feet. "I missed you too, lass, I like the hair."

She touched the ends and offered a wry smile. "It was time for a change."

"It looks good."

Cameron continued on to the table where Jayne now sat alone. Jon was the youngest of the group but he wasn't stupid. He had moved as soon as he'd seen Cam. Jayne didn't look the slightest bit disturbed by Rianne's enthusiastic greeting. It annoyed him that she wasn't even a little jealous, when just the fact that Jon sat next to her had his hackles raised. She watched him approach her with a slight smile. The same one that had annoyed him at the wedding, the one that said "*I know what you're doing*". He sat beside her, aware of the others chatting around them. She had a million questions swirling around in her head, most of which he didn't want to answer.

"I'm sorry about earlier. It won't happen again."

She quirked a brow at him. "Wanna bet?"

He frowned and she just smiled back at him. "You want to tell me why you called in the cavalry, Cam?" She held up a finger. "Think before you speak. You still haven't even given me a good explanation why anyone would be after me. There is no way on this earth I'm going to believe they just dropped in by chance. Mary said they run a security company but I don't buy it and I'm tired of being in the dark. And while you're thinking about that then you'd better think about how to explain your big friend over there." She glanced at Chris who still lounged near the doorway. "Because I already have some ideas of my own."

Cameron looked up at his friend, well aware the man had heard her though her voice was low. Chris shrugged. "It's Chris' story to tell, Jayne. If he decides to share it then that's up to him. As for the reason they're here," he gestured at the team as one by one they took seats at the table around them, "you're right, I called them." He paused while Mary sat mugs in front of them. "You know about Jack's brother, aye?"

"Yes, he disappeared."

"This afternoon, I got an e-mail from someone claiming to know where he is."

She looked from him to the serious faces around the table and frowned in puzzlement. "But that's good, isn't it? I assume you guys are here to go get him?"

Jonathon cleared his throat. "It's not that simple, Jayne." He looked at Cam, waiting for his nod of encouragement before he continued. "It could well be a trap. It's only been two days since someone tried to snatch you two and you've been holed up here ever since. This could just be an attempt to get Cam away from the house."

"Also, why now after all this time? There's nothing to suggest that Nick is even still alive," Rianne interjected. "What?" She glared at Ciaran when he nudged her. "It's the truth!"

"You spent way too much of your childhood with Mister Doom an' Gloom, darlin'." He glanced at Cameron.

"He's alive." The quiet statement came from Fynn. His American voice unmistakable though his face remained as expressionless as if he hadn't spoken.

Jayne looked at the faces of the people around her but no one looked surprised by the surety in Fynn's voice. She opened her mouth to ask how he knew only to close it abruptly when Cameron bumped her knee under the table. She looked at him and he shook his head slightly. *Right*, she scowled. One more damn mystery. She hadn't missed the fact that he had ignored her prod about explaining who was after them. But she kept her silence as he addressed the people seated at the table. She glanced up to see Fynn's wintry gaze on her. She shivered and he looked away.

"I'm still waiting for a reply to the message and I haven't been able to get any more information. I even pulled in some favors to check whether the libraries in the city have any kind of security surveillance in them. They do, but it's switched off in the daytime so no help there, even if we could find out which one was used."

Rianne launched into a detailed conversation with Cam about IP and Mac addresses and routing that made Jayne's eyes cross. Two computer geeks together. She tuned them out and studied the others at the table again. Ciaran and Jonathon were serious for once, talking in undertones. Christopher and Mary were talking about someone named Rebecca. From the occasional word she caught, Jayne gathered she was Chris' little girl. That surprised her, she couldn't quite imagine the big, silent man with a child. They were certainly a unique bunch. Chris most of all, though Fynn came a close second. It looked as though neither man spoke much. There was no way Cameron would convince her there was nothing unusual about them.

It was clear they all knew each other very well. Despite a slightly awkward first few minutes, Cameron had merged seamlessly with them. This was the most relaxed she had ever seen him. There was still a fine tension in him that she sensed had to do with her. He seemed to be hyper-aware of every move she made. There was an almost palpable connection between them and Jayne knew the others had picked up on it. She saw it in the glances exchanged between them.

When the conversation began to drift to a halt, Mary stood, yawning. "Well, boys and girls, I believe I'll go to bed. It's getting late."

Rianne stood. "I'll come with you, Mum."

There were murmurs of agreement around the table and one by one the others stood until only she and Cameron were left. She listened to their voices as they retrieved their bags and headed for their rooms.

"And then there were two." She turned to watch Cam, surprised when he didn't show any signs of leaving. Instead, he stared back at her, his expression quizzical.

"What?"

"You puzzle me, Jayne. Why do you find it so easy to believe in the fantastic when most people would accept any other explanation?"

"Yep, it drives Megan crazy too." She smiled and tried to answer his question. "I don't know why, Cam, it's just who I am, who I've always been, even as a child. Tell me about the monster under the bed and I'd want to know why the poor guy was hiding in there. I cried when I found out about the tooth fairy, and Santa Claus," she shook her head, "when I found out about him I was devastated."

"Who told you there were monsters under the bed?"

"Megan. I stole her coloring book and wouldn't give it back."

He shook his head and swung round in his seat 'til their knees touched. His mouth quirked in a slight smile. She had yet to see a full-fledged grin from him and wondered if the presence of his friends would change that. "This isnae a romance novel, you know, there's no guaranteed happy ending."

"Okay, now you're just trying to annoy me. I see you just fine, Cameron, and you look real enough to me. Besides, there's been way more frustration than satisfaction so far. You keep winding me up and letting me go!" He scowled at her and, encouraged, she leaned forward and purred against his lips. "The hero of a romance novel would have made sure I had at least one orgasm before now."

The longer she spent in his presence, the more twitchy she got. She didn't know how he made her feel this way when no one else ever had. She got to her feet, intending to make her exit. He grabbed her wrist and stood facing her.

"Woman, you drive me crazy! You dinnae ken what you're messin' with."

"Then tell me!" she hissed, their faces so close together she could see the darker gold striations in his eyes. There was anger and desire in his face and his body was shaking from the force of it. Abruptly he released her wrist. "All right! Goddammit! All right." He walked away and leaned against the granite counter with his back to her. Jayne took a deep breath and attempted to bring her racing pulse back under control.

"You've guessed most of it anyway…" She saw him visibly brace himself. "I'm a shapeshifter."

"I knew it! Jack too, right? And your friends? This is brilliant!"

Cameron turned, disbelief on his face. "Doesn't this even shock you a wee bit?"

"Why would it? It's not as if I didn't know already. Can I see you change?"

"No!" He raked his hand through his hair. "It disnae work like that. Look, sit down, okay?" He went to the other end of the kitchen and rummaged in cupboards, producing a bottle of whiskey and two glasses. He sat, poured them both a generous portion before beginning to speak again.

"Okay, here it is. I'm a feline shapeshifter, so were my parents and so are many of my friends. We're not freaks or monsters. What we are is a separate race with a different culture and history. A history that as far as anyone can trace begins right here in Scotland. We live relatively normal lives.

Except that puberty for us, along with everythin' else, means our first transformation."

"That has to suck." Especially for him, since that's when he'd lost his parents.

"Aye, it does. But we get plenty of time to recover from it since we don't change again until around the age of thirty, give or take a few years. That's when we have to deal with a new hell. It's called the mating cycle."

"And you'd be thirty…?"

"Three."

"Ah."

He raised his glass in a mocking toast and lifted it to his lips then put it down again with a grimace. "The matin' cycle is a polite way of saying that the animal that lives inside me wants—no, *demands*—a mate. So I get an increased sex drive and in return I gradually lose my appetite and my ability to sleep. Until I give in to the demand."

"And if you don't give in?"

"Then, in theory, I could eventually starve to death. Though I dinnae think anyone has let it get that far, not for a long time anyway."

She looked at the cold, untouched mug of chocolate he had left sitting on the table and the glass of whiskey he had yet to drink from. Remembered all the missed meals in the last few days. And worried. "So, why don't you just find a woman?"

"Oh, that's the best part. See not just any woman will do, only the ones who are genetically compatible. There's always a very strong sexual pull between shifters and those women and, during the matin' cycle, we just cannae get it up for anyone else. Aside from the obvious," he gestured to the bulge of his erection under his jeans. "There are other signs that *you* are one of the ones who are compatible. That birthmark you have on the inside of your thigh, the one shaped like a cat's paw is one."

Her hand immediately went to cover the mark though it was under her jeans.

"And another is the fact that I can hear some of your thoughts and feelings, especially if we are close to each other."

Jayne flushed crimson as she remembered all the lustful daydreams she had had about Cameron in the last couple of days. She took a large gulp of the whiskey. It burned all the way down, making her eyes water.

"Oh aye, I definitely caught some of those. You havnae made it easy to stay away from you, Jayne."

"Then why did you?"

"Because if I take you, make you my mate…then we'd be stuck with each other for good. And if one of us decides we dinnae like the other," he shrugged, "too bad."

There was a bitterness in his voice that didn't match his matter-of-fact words and Jayne wondered at its source. "You still haven't told me how all this is related to you changing. I take it that it has something to do with this mating cycle?" *And why do you hate the idea so much?*

"It has everything to do with it. It's just hard to explain to someone who cannae feel what I feel. I dinnae hate what I am, Jayne, although what I've said might make you think that. I just hate what I have to do to someone else so that I can be complete." He spun his glass in slow circles on the table. "I could give all the sensible, reasonable explanations for what we are and what we do. Especially when it comes to the matin' bond. Scent, pheromones, biological markers…but at the root of it all is magic." The tips of his ears flushed red, signaling his embarrassment. His obvious discomfort made Jayne want to hug him but she sat where she was, worried that she might put him off.

"We all have our own theories about how it works and everyone is told a slightly different version as a child but it basically always comes down to the same thing. The magic in me recognizes the dormant magic in you and it needs it. But in order to bring it to the surface, it has to feed it with some of the energy that is usually used to control the cat. It happens through direct contact, we do have some control over when it happens but it takes concentration. Here." He reached out his hand. "Give me your hand and close your eyes. Concentrate, tell me what you feel."

Jayne felt his hand close over hers. "Warmth, your skin on mine, your heartbeat...mine...and something else. A tingling...very faint, like pins and needles." He released her hand abruptly and she opened her eyes and saw his fingers trembling.

"We call it the *Ceangal*, it's Gaelic for bond. It's an instinct—like an automatic reflex—and the longer you put it off, the harder it gets to control. Once that link is made I have no say over where or when I change into the cat until the energy is equalized and the bond is completed. And if I don't complete it, the changes come more often until, eventually, I just wouldn't change back from the feline form."

"Which would really suck."

"Oh aye."

He really was a very attractive man in a rough-around-the-edges sort of way. He had relaxed a bit, slouching in the chair so that his long legs stretched out under the table in a graceful sprawl. His golden eyes reflected the color of the whiskey in his glass and his tawny hair gleamed under the bright lights of the kitchen.

"Okay, I'm getting that it's no picnic for you but you also said you didn't like what you'd have to do to someone else, so spill."

"At first, there's not much effect on the female except that the mental link gets a little stronger. But once the couple completes the bond, she would become like he is and they would remain a mated couple for the rest of their lives."

"Wait a minute. Megan is a shapeshifter!?" Jayne gaped at him, astonished that her friend had hidden something so major from her. "I'm going to kill her!"

"Jayne, try to focus for a minute. Did you no' hear any of what Ah just said?" Cameron's accent thickened.

"You're damn right and I can't believe she didn't tell me!"

"Forget that for a minute. Ah said that they would be stuck with each other for the rest of their lives. Can you imagine bein' tied to somebody you didnae like forever? Worse, someone you still wanted to fuck even though you hated them?"

Jayne shoved Megan's duplicity aside for the moment and considered Cameron's words. She watched him stand. Pace. Even back at the wedding—it seemed like a lifetime ago—she had been drawn to him. Despite his attitude and, she admitted, maybe even a little because of it. In this very short time, she had begun to see the man underneath. He was intriguing, annoying, complicated, fascinating…hurt. The more she saw of him the more she wanted him and, despite his prickly demeanor, she suspected her feelings were returned. She could think of no one else she'd rather be stuck with forever.

"I like you just fine, Cameron. More than like you, actually."

He sighed and stared at her from across the room, worry and a guarded hope in his eyes. "Ah…I like you, too. But it's not as easy as that for me, Jayne. I need to be sure, so do you."

He walked out, leaving her sitting alone in the kitchen with a thousand thoughts flying around in her head.

Chapter Nine

ᔕ

Cameron lay back on his bed and wondered what the hell had just happened. He didn't know whether to be glad or worried that Jayne now knew it all. Perhaps this would be all she'd finally need to keep her distance. Only he wasn't sure that was what he wanted anymore. She was an amazing woman. Full of fire and courage and so beautiful that she took his breath away every time he looked at her.

He had been so sure he knew what his beliefs were regarding the *Dearbh Ceangal* but now they were all mixed up with his growing feelings for Jayne. It might be a long time before he was confident about it but he was willing to take the chance now. If there was the smallest possibility of a future with her...he wanted it. Somewhere in the last couple of days a tiny seed of hope had taken root in him, but it had taken Chris with his brutal honesty to make him see it.

Cam felt her presence in the hallway just as he had resigned himself to yet another sleepless night alone. He had to force himself not to rush to the door. He waited, not reading anything from her but a quiet resolution as she walked into the softly lit room. She stepped closer and his head spun with a dizzy relief as he took her in his arms. The energy of the mating bond washed over him and for the first time he savored it.

"I've decided." She smiled slowly, mischief lighting her green eyes. "I hope you're ready for this, Cameron."

"Lass, Ah was ready the minute Ah saw you. In a church, no less. Ah was just waiting for the lightning to strike me down."

He pulled the tie from her hair, letting it drop to the floor and swept his fingers though the long red strands. Jayne tilted her face up to his and he kissed her. A feather-soft pressure of his lips to hers that became nibbles, then demands, until she opened her mouth to him and let him devour her. Arousal flared to life, quick, hot, hard. The long-denied *Ceangal* soared in its wake, sending stronger waves of energy coursing over him, through him. Demanding, insistent, *take her*. They parted long enough for her to strip his sweater from him and run her hands over his chest. She drew back slightly, met his gaze and whispered, "Will I feel it?"

"Ah dinnae know."

She nudged him back toward the bed, pushed him back onto it and pulled off her own sweater. "Let's find out." She took a wrapped condom from her pocket and tossed it to him. Cam caught it one-handed and smiled at her. "Should Ah be offended that you thought Ah would be this easy?" He shifted up until he lay fully on the soft mattress and watched as she unbuttoned her jeans and pushed them down and off along with her shoes. She laughed, clearly enjoying the role reversal. "I don't think you're easy, sweetheart, I was just being hopeful."

When she joined him on the bed, she wore nothing but her sea foam-colored bra and panties. Her skin was creamy perfection but for the chocolate-brown birthmark high up on the inside of her thigh. One larger, vaguely oval, smudge orbited by four smaller ones. It marked her as his in a tangible way. He ran his fingers over it and shivered.

Take her.

His breath shuddered in his chest as she crawled up the length of his body, fiery hair loose and tousled around her face. Pale skin luminous in the soft light of the bedside lamp. A stunning contrast against the dark, masculine furnishings of the bedroom. She smiled wickedly at him and paused to unbutton his jeans. Cam lifted his hips and allowed her to pull them down and off. His erection sprang free and he thought he might explode from excitement alone. Then she touched him. Just a brush of her fingertips at first, up and down the length of his cock while she watched his face. When she closed her fist around his swollen flesh, he gasped.

Instead of stroking him, she began to gently squeeze and release him, moving her thumb in small circles over the sensitive head. He sucked in air through gritted teeth, his whole world suddenly centered on her face and the pressure of her hand on his cock. He was helpless to prevent his hips from rising from the bed in an attempt to thrust against her hand. She merely moved with him, bringing him to the brink of orgasm but denying him the release he knew was a mortifyingly few strokes away. His hard-on pulsed against her palm in time with his heartbeat.

"Ahh, fuck me," he groaned.

Jayne chuckled. "I intend to." She released him, raising her hand to her lips and licked the evidence of his arousal from her thumb. He reached for her, feeling his hands tremble and not caring. She moved with a liquid grace, her green eyes hot on his, her mouth pink and swollen from his kiss. Jayne gripped his hands in hers and straddled him so that his cock nestled between the cheeks of her ass, against the silk of her panties.

Take her.

Cameron moaned, finding himself suddenly short of breath. He could feel the familiar prickling in his fingertips that signaled the *Ceangal* and struggled for control. *Take her.* When she leaned forward, letting her hair fall down around their faces and breathed against his lips, "Do it now." When he let go, let the magic spill out of him into her, registering the sharp pain in his hands as it did. Colors spilled around them, from her and from him. Red, blue, brown, pink, silver, gold. They swirled together and faded and then there was only Jayne.

His *fior cèile.*

"It didn't hurt," she whispered.

He kissed her again, drawing her tongue into his mouth and letting her take his in turn. He felt her arousal, knew she wanted him with a passion rivaling his own. The thin silk of her panties tore easily in his hands, revealing a triangle of red pubic hair. He felt lightheaded, shaky but when she rocked her hips and he felt her wet heat against him, it didn't seem to matter. He reached behind her and unfastened her bra, tossed it away and let her breasts spill free into his hands. When he stroked her nipples with his thumbs, her moans made his cock burn.

Cameron rolled, taking her with him so that he was nestled between her legs. He bent his head to her breasts, suckling at her until her hands fisted in his hair and pulled his mouth back to hers. His fingers found her wet and ready and he caressed her folds with his damp fingertips, spreading her moisture until he could push inside her with one finger, then two. Thrusting as he stroked and circled her clitoris, Jayne moaned and clung to him, kissing him as though she wanted to crawl inside him. She came in a rush, wetting his hand with her release. While she was still clenching with orgasm, he withdrew his fingers, put the condom on and entered her.

"Cameron!"

Her body gave way reluctantly to his. Slick, wet, warmth enveloped his cock, making him grit his teeth. She wrapped her legs around his hips and he felt her internal muscles tighten and release around him as she adjusted to his girth. Cam pressed his forehead against her, breath rasping in his throat as he tried to hold on. But when she rocked her hips against him, he knew he was lost. "Jayne, love. It's been too long, Ah'm sorry…Ah can't hold on."

She tilted her head and nipped at his chin then took his hands in hers. "Don't."

They began to move together, hands and bodies locked together. His heart pounded and he felt the blood rushing in his ears. Driving forward as she arched back to meet him. He felt the approach of her climax in the tension of her body, heard it in the quickening of her breath. She dug her nails into his hands and held him tight to her as she cried out her release. The clench and spasm of her body tipped him over the edge and he followed her, spilling his seed.

Cameron collapsed beside her, exhausted and fought to catch his breath. He disposed of the condom, then pulled Jayne into his arms and flipped the edge of the duvet over them. The lightheadedness he had felt earlier returned with a vengeance now that his body was sated. He recognized it now as a side effect from starting the *Ceangal* and knew his body needed to rest. It was the last thing he wanted to do. His *fíor cèile* was snug against his side, her head resting beneath his collarbone. She was playing with the hair on his chest, following its trail down to his abdomen. He wanted to pull her over him, explore her without the urgency of their first mating. But his body felt heavy and even as he tried to fight it, it worsened until it was all he could do to lift his arm to caress her. As he opened his mouth to explain, sleep stole over him.

Lying in his arms, Jayne felt the moment his body relaxed into slumber and smiled. It seemed that as well as finding out what besides anger deepened his Scottish accent, she had cured his insomnia. His loose-limbed sprawl took up a good portion of the huge bed. One corner of the sheet covered his sex, leaving the rest of his body gloriously displayed, his golden coloring contrasting sharply with the royal blue bedding. She ran her hand over the hard planes of his chest and abdomen, feeling his broad chest rising and falling as he breathed, and toyed with the fine mat of dark blond hair there. Petting him like the big cat he claimed he would become. She had been right, he definitely had a six-pack. His body was completely relaxed and she could still trace its shape. Her brow creased in a frown as she realized she could also trace his ribs.

How far would he have let himself go before giving in? Given his stubbornness and his past history, she thought he might well have gone all the way. Oh, she knew Mary would have done everything in her power to help him and Jayne suspected the woman had more training than she let on but there was only so much you could do for someone who wouldn't—or couldn't—eat. The thought of him locked away in this house slowly fading away was unbearable. Thankfully if what he had said was true it wouldn't be an issue anymore.

She didn't feel any different physically, didn't even know if she should. It was hard to believe her whole life had changed in these last couple of hours. And it had. Even if nothing came of this "*Ceangal*", she still believed she and this beautiful, complicated man had a connection unlike anything she had ever felt. Despite her easy acceptance, it was a fantastic story. Part of her was still waiting for someone to jump out and yell "Surprise!" But even if they did—and that would be terribly disappointing—she was exactly where she wanted to be. *This* was the magic she had been trying to find all of her life.

* * * * *

Outside in the woods Henry was praying for some magic of his own. The snow had stopped and as the sky had cleared the temperature had dropped. A bright moon lit the night, turning the snow a luminous blue-white and making the shadows under the trees where he lay thicker. He had a very bad feeling about this. This was never intended to be a surveillance mission. He had expected to go in grab the targets and go. But suddenly a man who hadn't had a visitor in months had a houseful and he was stuck out here freezing his bollocks off.

It wasn't his turn to be on watch but he dared not take his eyes off the house. The lights had gone off one by one until only one window was lit by a soft glow. Henry had watched through the conservatory windows as the people in the house had gathered in the kitchen. He would have sold his soul for a long-range listening device or at least some lip-reading abilities, especially when Murray and the woman had been alone together. Now the couple was in the bedroom and had been for hours. It didn't take a rocket scientist to figure out what was going on. He hadn't seen the telltale flare of heat yet on the thermal imager that would signify that either of them had changed and all he could do was wait.

* * * * *

At some point during her musings, Jayne joined Cameron in sleep. When she opened her eyes, the window was letting in gray morning light. She was too warm. Cameron lay curled on his side facing her, heat radiated from him like a furnace and he had thrown the duvet off so that she lay under a double layer. His chin was covered in a heavy growth of stubble and his brows were lowered in a ferocious frown, though he continued to snore gently. She smiled, remembering how she had decided that it must be his default expression. It seemed he even did it in his sleep. Gently she eased out from under the covers and out of the bed, trying not to disturb him. She wanted to shower before he woke then maybe get a breakfast tray that they could share in bed. If the man hadn't enjoyed a meal in two years, she was going to make this first one memorable.

Since the water felt heavenly, she lingered a few minutes longer than she had planned. She had whisker burn on her jaw and on her breasts. Her skin felt sensitive in the way that only came after making love. As though every nerve ending was awake and anticipating the next caress. Cameron was a big man in every way and she felt deliciously achy between her legs as a result. Jayne shivered as she passed the cloth over her delicate flesh. She couldn't wait to feel him there again. Maybe they could wait for breakfast. She stepped out of the shower and dried herself quickly, wrapping her body in a towel. She walked back into the bedroom, mind already filled with him and with possibilities.

"Eeep!" *Except this one.*

Pacing up and down in front of the bed was a lion. A big, huge, enormous lion. His fur was the same rich gold as Cam's hair, his mane and the tuft on his twitching tail a few shades darker. Powerful muscles slid beneath his hide as he walked on paws the size of dinner plates. Jayne clutched the towel tighter to her breasts and realized she never had asked what kind of cat Cameron was.

No need to now.

The cat had frozen at her exclamation and now stood staring at her with familiar amber-colored eyes. *Was he even in there? Was he in control? Did he recognize her or would the lion just see her as prey and attack her? All good questions, Jayne, but a bit late now!* She tried to push it away but fear crept in insidiously. He moved toward her and she took an involuntary step back. Regretting it instantly when he turned and bounded from the room.

"Cameron! Wait!"

She raced after him, nearly running headlong into Jonathon and Ciaran on the first-floor landing. She skidded to a halt and looked around but there was no sign of Cam.

"Which way did he go?"

Jonathon gaped at her and pointed down the stairs wordlessly before training his eyes somewhere over her left shoulder. Ciaran gave her a lopsided grin, brown eyes twinkling as they wandered the length of her body.

"Jayne, my darlin', that's a very becoming outfit."

Jayne looked down at herself and felt her cheeks going scarlet as she realized she was still only wearing a towel. A towel that was feeling smaller by the minute. *Hell.*

Ciaran cocked an eyebrow at her, still grinning. "What's up, love, cat got yer ton—Oof!" The force of Jonathon's elbow made him double over. "Now that was uncalled for, mate, I was only asking the lass a simple question."

"Excuse me." She gathered together the shreds of her dignity—a difficult thing when you had a draft blowing on your bare backside—and went back upstairs to dress.

By the time she walked into the kitchen, Jayne was fully clothed. Wet hair tied back in a ponytail, dignity more or less intact. She couldn't remember the last time she had been that embarrassed. If the guys had any heart, they would pretend she hadn't stood in front of them almost naked. That way she could just forget it had ever happened.

"You look a bit warmer this time, love."

Or not.

Ciaran grinned wickedly at her from his seat at the table. There was a pot of tea in front of him and a cup at his hand. The glass expanse behind him displayed a scene straight out of a Christmas card. The snow had stopped finally, leaving behind a smooth white expanse. It stretched back from the patio at the kitchen door all the way down to the tree line and coated the pine trees in a heavy blanket. Jayne longed to explore it but first, she had to set things straight with her new…what? Fiancé? Husband? Mate?

"Where's Cameron?"

"I've no idea."

"Come on, Ciaran, I know it's a big house but it's not that big and he's a bit hard to miss at the moment."

His grin faded. "Give him some time, Jayne, he's got a lot to deal with."

"*He's* got a lot to deal with?"

"Aside from the fact that we have someone out there who tried to kidnap you two just a few days ago and findin' out Nick could still be alive. Now he has to deal with the whole *Ceangal* issue. You don't understand how big that is. When his father died, Cameron swore he would never take a mate and now he's disregarded everything he believes and done just that. I assume that this morning was the first time he shifted?" He paused for her nod of confirmation. "Then it's the first time he's shifted since he was sixteen and even then it only happened once. That's a lot...and before you say a word, I know you have a lot to deal with too but unlike women," he smiled at her, "who like to share all their problems, we men prefer beer and solitude. Not necessarily in that order."

"What order?" Jonathon ambled through the kitchen door, carrying a large, intriguingly familiar-looking, brown paper-wrapped package.

"Beer and solitude, your lordship," Ciaran replied.

"Ah, the finer things in life. Just add a good computer game in there and you have a happy man."

Jayne smiled at him. "I thought you would say football."

"No! You need company for that."

He sat the package on the table and Jayne's fingers itched to open it. "Is that what I think it is?"

"I suspect so, Cam asked us to pick them up for you on the way."

Her heart gave a foolish little flutter and she eagerly tore off the brown paper, smiling when she saw the five canvases and a large sketch pad. He seemed to be determined that she go back to her art. It had been so long. Maybe later she would try some sketching. She looked at the two men watching her, lord knows there was certainly plenty of inspiration around here.

"Thank you."

Jonathon shrugged good-naturedly. "Don't thank us, we were only doing as we were asked. What were you two talking about so intently when I came in?"

"Now, Jon, mate, how many times do I have to tell you what curiosity did to the cat?"

"Very funny, Ciaran. Chase any cars lately?"

Jayne listened to the two men with half an ear. Maybe Ciaran was right and she should let Cameron have his space. Not too much though, she wanted to make sure he knew she was okay with the whole lion thing. She did have one pressing question though. It had occurred to her when she was getting dressed. She'd rather ask Cam but since he was hiding…

"Guys, when do I change into a cat?"

The two men fell abruptly silent.

"I mean, Cameron told me I would but he didn't go into any detail last night before we were…sidetracked." She felt her face heat. "Should I be watching out for unusual hair growth and cravings for raw meat?"

Ciaran raised his eyebrows and looked at Jonathon. "Think you're the best person to answer that one, your lordship, it's not my area of expertise."

"That's an unflattering description of my future." Jonathon shook his head and grinned, his green-gold eyes twinkling. "You won't change yet, Cameron hasn't completed the *Ceangal*." He held up a hand to still her questions. "He started it when he touched you and merged your energies."

"And now he starts to change into a cat, a very *big* cat."

"Right. Now he has a few days, perhaps as long as a week, to complete the bond by introducing the shapeshifter genes into your system."

Jayne frowned at him. "Basically, you mean, he has to infect me." She felt her cheeks color. "Is this like some kind of magical sexually transmitted disease?"

Ciaran roared with laughter and Jonathon glared at him. "No. It's a blood exchange. It only takes a tiny amount and it doesn't matter how it's done, most of us prefer old-fashioned way though. Less clinical. Just prick your partner's finger and kiss it better and then let them do the same."

"You mean drink it?" He nodded and watched her warily. "Wow…shades of Dracula." She paused, considering it. "Okay, I can handle that. Thanks, Jon."

She gathered up the canvases and sketch pad and stood to leave, smiling at their surprised expressions. "I can't believe he didn't tell me! That he'd risk himself like that. If you should see Cameron, tell him he has an hour and then I'm coming after him, no matter how many legs he's standing on."

* * * * *

From between the slats of the blinds, the professor watched the girl get into her compact white car, such a little brown mouse. He sneered as he watched her drive off. He had thought she would have more promise, especially after the loss of her parents had given him control of her. The man standing behind him shuffled his feet uncomfortably and he turned to face him.

"Is everything prepared?" He did not like this disruption to his normal routine but it was a necessary evil, he would reap the benefits of it in the end.

"They're getting him ready now, sir. Should I have security follow her?"

"No, let her go. She's not going far."

Such a shame, she was entirely her father's daughter. Things could have been accomplished so much more easily if she had been a little more…flexible. But he had known her morals would prevail. Had, in fact, counted on it.

He still had plans for his niece.

Chapter Ten

ဢ

Cameron groaned and lay on Chris' bedroom floor, shuddering as the remnants of pain from the transformation ebbed away. His friend draped a towel over his body and crouched at his side, setting a glass of water on the floor.

"Those shifts really are a bitch before you do the blood exchange, aren't they?"

He laughed shakily and tried to take stock of his body. His senses, though they had already been acute, had improved even more. Everything was sharper, clearer. "That's an understatement, I feel like I've been set on fire and then turned inside out. Twice."

Cameron took the offered hand and let Chris help him sit up, towel draped over his lap. He pushed sweat-dampened hair out of his face and downed the glass of water. He had spent just over two hours in one of the first-floor parlors avoiding Jayne. Fighting against the cat's determination to go to his mate had been more difficult than he had expected. At first, Jayne's fear had been enough to give him the strength to run from her but that had only lasted so long. The cat's natural instinct was to pursue, not flee, and the battle between the cat's desires and his own will had left him exhausted. It had been all he could do to stay in the room, only daring to move next door to the sanctuary of Chris' bedroom when he felt the heat of the change coming again. He was lucky Chris had left his door ajar, he had just made it inside when the pain had swept through him.

"So, you decided to take the plunge. Congratulations." Chris got to his feet and started opening drawers. He tossed a T-shirt and a pair of sweatpants to him.

"Dinnae congratulate me yet, she freaked out when she saw the cat."

Chris looked at him, brows raised in surprise. "She freaked out?"

"Well, okay," he admitted grudgingly. "She didnae freak out exactly, but she was afraid of me, Chris, I felt it."

"Hell, Cam, you have to give her a chance to get used to the idea…yourself too."

"Aye, mebbe." He climbed shakily to his feet and immediately felt a little disorientated at being so high above the ground again. Chris watched him silently as he leaned against the bed and pulled on the borrowed clothes. "I need to check my e-mail. Thanks, man."

"No problem, just don't leave it too long, Cam."

Cameron laughed softly. "Not very long ago, I said something very similar to Jack, only I wisnae so polite."

Chris grinned, displaying his elongated canines and opened the door for him. "Karma bites you on the ass, eh, my friend?"

He stopped by his bedroom to shower and dress and managed to get to his office without encountering his mate though he could feel her nearby. It was only a matter of time before she checked back here. It was odd. For years, he had been told about and read about the *Ceangal*. Even seen it in action, but experiencing it was nothing like he had expected. It was as though a part of his mind was always aware of Jayne's presence or, presumably, her absence. He wasn't ready to face her yet. When he had seen and *felt* her fear of him this morning, all he been able to think of was his mother. She had feared the transformation, hated everything about it, including his father. He couldn't bear to have Jayne think of him that way and he was very much afraid of what he might feel from her when she caught up with him.

If that made him a coward then so be it.

Cam sat at his computer with a sigh and clicked open his e-mail program, waiting while his new messages downloaded. He looked at his hands as they worked the keyboard. It was hard to believe they had been paws less than twenty minutes ago. How long did he have before they would be that way again? He had thought he had remembered what it was like to shift from his experience in his teens but he hadn't been prepared at all. Time had dulled the memory of the pain.

He *had* remembered that the cat was very much a separate being, at least until after the *Ceangal* was completed. That hadn't been an issue when he was a teenager, he had been quite happy to let the instincts of the lion take over. They hadn't been so very different from his own, basic, primitive and ultimately as self-centered as only a teen could be. And he had been more troubled than most.

It had been a wild ride, hunting in the woods around the house, learning the scents and sounds of his territory. Experiencing the world from a completely new perspective. As a result, he hadn't realized how difficult it would be to fight against the cat. It had taken almost every ounce of his concentration to keep it from going to Jayne. It didn't care whether she feared it.

That only made the chase better.

Before he could consider that consequences of *that* notion, the computer chimed to let him know his mail was ready. Anticipation pushed his heart into his throat as he spied a familiar sender. Quickly he opened it and scanned the note, tears stung his eyes as he read the word "*alive*". As promised, there were directions included for Nick's whereabouts. The location was vaguely familiar, a few hours' drive from here and isolated. It could be a trap. Cameron knew that but, lord, he wanted to believe it. Hope crept in despite his attempt to remain skeptical. He printed off the e-mail, grabbing the page and heading for the library to find a map.

As he reached the foot of the stairs Jayne stepped into his path, her determined expression changing to curiosity when she looked at his face.

"What is it?" Her gaze fell on the page in his hand. "You heard something."

"Aye."

He wanted to pull her into his arms, share his hope and his fears with her. Instead he brushed past her, hearing her fall into step behind him. She bombarded him with relief and hope and worry and excitement. Emotion on top of emotion until he couldn't distinguish them. Until he couldn't tell which were hers and which were his anymore. From the first moment they met, he had been more aware of Jayne's emotions than her thoughts and apparently the bond had intensified the empathy. He had known that the *Ceangal* could take that direction. He just hadn't expected the effects to be so strong yet. Doing his best to block it, he led the way into the library.

He wasn't surprised to find the large, comfortable room already occupied. As was his custom, Fynn was sprawled in one of the armchairs by the fireplace reading. He glanced up as they entered and closed the paperback and laid it facedown on his leather-clad knee.

"I have a location, I need a map."

"On the table." Cameron had spent too long around Fynn to be surprised that he already had the appropriate map ready. The man sometimes just *knew* things, though he didn't always know why. It had to be frustrating as hell but there were times when Cam suspected he enjoyed being a mysterious bastard. He was just thankful that Jayne seemed to have missed the significance. They didn't need any more complications. The other man stood, leaving the book on the seat and turned his pale eyes on Jayne briefly. "Congratulations. I'll get the rest of the guys. We'll wait in your office."

She waited silently until the door closed. "Is that a romance?" she asked incredulously and picked up Fynn's book. "It *is*. The scary, quiet guy reads romances? I feel a whole lot less intimidated now."

"I wouldnae," he warned. "And please, dinnae mention it to him. I havnae got time to clean up the mess."

"Okaaaay." She put the book back on the chair. "Does everyone know what happened last night?"

He slowly opened the door to her emotions again, feeling her curiosity, her embarrassment and an undercurrent of desire.

But no fear.

Something inside him eased at the realization and he shrugged. "They can feel the difference in me. And even if they couldnae, Ciaran and Jon would have told the rest. They need to know, the *Ceangal* is unpredictable." He lowered his eyes. "So am I when it comes to my mate, if anythin' were to threaten you…it's a weakness at the moment."

"Cam, I need to explain about this morning." He started to speak and she shook her head and moved to stand in front of him. "I won't wait any longer… I wasn't afraid of you." He gave a short laugh, rich with disbelief. "Fine, I was, but it's not every day you come out of the bathroom and find an enormous lion in front of you! And let me tell you, you're a big cat! It kind of causes an immediate reaction, I had no idea what to expect. I didn't even know if you would recognize me!" She put her hand on his chest and he felt the contact all the way to his toes, her sincerity washed through him. "I'm sorry. Apparently I'm not as open-minded as I thought I was."

"Ah did recognize you." Cameron's accent thickened from the heat of her touch. "Ah'll *always* recognize you, no matter what form I take. So does the cat, he won't hurt you."

"So he is different from you?"

"He's a part of me…but during the *Ceangal*, he gets stronger and my ability to control him is weakened. No matter what happens from here on, Jayne, Ah'm never goin' to be the same again. Either he'll win control—or I will—but either way, he's always goin' to be nearer the surface. If you cannae accept that then tell me now, before things go any further."

"You mean before you finish what you started. You should have told me about completing the bond, Cam. You have to know I would never have let you risk your humanity like this."

He scowled at her. "I'm going to kill those two. It's just…after this morning…Ah wanted to give you a little more time. Ah wanted you to be able to make your decision without worryin' about me."

The need to touch her surged again as she frowned at him and this time he gave in to it. Caressing her cheek with his fingertips and cupping her face in his hand. He smoothed his thumb over the softness of her lips and she parted them to take it into her mouth, sucking gently. Cam groaned as his cock surged to life.

"Cameron, let's go, pal!" Ciaran's voice echoed down the hall.

Reluctantly, he drew away from her. "I have to go, we need to make a plan so that they can move quickly."

"They? You're not going with them?"

"No, Ah'm not leavin' you here alone. Besides, we have unfinished business of our own."

"You should go, he's your friend. I'll be fine."

"Ah *will not* leave you unprotected!"

"Then let one of the others stay, Cam… If this was Megan, I know I'd want to be there to rescue her."

"You're right, Ah do. But Ah trust the team to get Nick out safely. Right now Ah *need* to be here with you, Jayne."

He kissed her gently and picked up the map.

"Cam?" He stopped. "I've had enough time."

Jayne watched him stride out of the room again, only this time on two legs instead of four. Lord, he was frustrating. Why did men have to make things more complicated than they were? Why couldn't he get it into his head? She had made her decision last night and she wasn't going to change her mind, certainly not because she got a little bit of a surprise. Maybe he just needed a little positive reinforcement. There was no reason she couldn't continue with her plans from this morning. After all, Cam was certain to need some distraction since he was going to be stuck here with her. She didn't think he could have eaten yet, not when she was chasing him all over the house like a bizarre reverse game of cat and mouse.

The kitchen was filled with the delicious scent of a roast cooking, though Mary was nowhere to be seen. Jayne started searching cupboards and fridge for suitable supplies. She wrinkled her nose in mingled sympathy and distaste when she came across one filled with high-protein, high-calorie meal substitutes. If that was what he had been living on, she was definitely going to make sure he never had to look at them again. No one should be subjected to that.

"Good afternoon, Jayne, pet."

Jayne turned toward the voice, automatically hiding the can of whipped cream in her hand behind her back. "Mary, hi!"

The housekeeper smiled. "Too late, love, I already saw it and your reaction tells me everything I need to know about what you intend to do with it. That poor boy isn't going to know what hit him. Congratulations, by the way."

Jayne silently cursed her fair complexion as she felt her cheeks heat. It was like being caught naked by her boyfriend's mother. Of course, it could be worse, she could actually *be* naked. "Oh lord, can't we just pretend you have no idea what's going on?"

"Where's the fun in that?" She grinned and her expression turned wistful. "David, Rianne's father, loved to play."

"What happened to him?" Jayne shook her head, seeing the sadness on the other woman's face. "I'm sorry, you don't have to answer that."

"Och, it's fine, love, it was a long time ago… He was killed in an accident when Rianne was very young. I was a nurse at the time and found myself alone with a young child. I couldn't keep up with the demands of working in a big hospital and I found I wanted to spend more time with my daughter. The job here was a godsend. I even got to work one or two days a week at the local clinic. I still do as a matter of fact, I'm going there this afternoon." She smiled, shrugging off the memories of the past and took the can of cream. "We can do much better than that."

She rummaged through another cupboard and handed Jayne two plastic bottles. She eyed the contents with amusement, chocolate sauce and honey. "Does Cam have a sweet tooth?"

"He certainly used to before and now he has his *Dearbh Ceangal*, I imagine he will again." She produced a small picnic basket from another cupboard and put a bottle of soda from the fridge inside then turned to take the roast beef from the oven.

"*Derav Kea al.* Cameron said that the first night we arrived, what does it mean? I know the second part means bond."

Mary quickly masked her frown and began buttering thick slices of bread for sandwiches. "I think that is something Cameron should talk to you about, dear." She held up a hand as Jayne opened her mouth to protest. "Don't worry, it's nothing bad but it's something he'll talk to you about when he's ready. Now, why don't you take this upstairs, they shouldn't be too much longer. His room would be best, yours is just too white." She stopped.

Before she could utter another word, Jayne found herself ushered out of the door, picnic basket in hand.

Chapter Eleven

The sleek, muscular lines of the big cat seemed to flow from the charcoal as Jayne pictured him in her mind's eye. It felt so good to be drawing again. Why had she stopped? It seemed impossible now that she had let herself retreat from the world the way she had. She had Cameron Murray to thank for giving her back her life. Okay, and maybe Jack and Megan a little too. If Jack hadn't sought out Megan, Jayne would probably still be in the same little rut. Stuck in a job she hated, avoiding her boss's groping hands. Going home at night to sit with her nose in a book while her paints gathered dust under the bed and life passed her by. It looked as if Cam and she were birds of a feather — *or cats of a fur?* — in that one. They both had their reasons for stepping away from other people. Although, admittedly, Cam's reasons made hers look a little superficial.

Distantly, she heard doors closing and engines rumble to life as Cam's friends left and looked around to make sure everything was ready. It was time to lay everything out in the open. Enough secrets. She had spread a plaid blanket on the thick blue-gray carpet in his bedroom and set out the sandwiches and drinks. Everything else she had left in the basket near at hand. Jayne set aside the sketchpad and leaned back against the foot of the oak bed. The edges of Cam's soft cotton robe parted around her bare legs and she smiled in anticipation. She had expected him to call out for her so it was a surprise when moments later the bedroom door opened.

"Hi. How did you know I was here?"

His eyes swept over her, lingering on her legs before moving back to her face. An uncertain smile kicked up the corner of his mouth.

"I'll always know where you are," his eyes flicked toward the blanket and the picnic, "and I followed my nose."

She studied him, intrigued. "Literally? You mean like a bloodhound?"

He frowned at her and stepped into the room, closing the door behind him. "Please, I'm much better than any canine."

"How could you possibly smell these sandwiches over the scent of the roast in the kitchen?"

"Who said anything about the sandwiches?"

"Are you saying I stink?"

"I'm saying you smell wonderful, like fresh spring air. I'd recognize your scent anywhere." After a moment's hesitation, he sat cross-legged on the blanket opposite her. "What's all this in aid of?"

"It's a celebration, didn't we just get engaged last night?"

He studied her a moment, head tilted as though listening to voices she couldn't hear. Uncertainty was replaced by relief. "I guess we did. But there are things you don't know yet, things you havenae seen."

Happiness swept through her along with a relief of her own. "I know, and that is going to change right now. I am tired of being the only one not in on the secret."

His stomach growled loudly and Jayne laughed at his embarrassment. "But while you talk, why don't you eat." She smiled at him. "You're going to need the energy, we both have a lot of time to make up for and I have plans."

He paused in the act of reaching for the plate and looked at her, eyes hot. "Ah can eat later."

"Nuh-uh. Eat and talk, mister. You can start with your parents and then tell me about the *Dearbh Ceangal*."

He sat back, sandwich in hand and Jayne was sorry to see his face had resumed its usual somber lines. As fond as she had grown of his frown, she really wanted to see less of it, but there was time for that.

"There isn't much to tell," he said matter-of-factly. "My mother hated my father, was terrified and disgusted by what he was. By what he made her. When I was fifteen, she killed herself to escape it."

"Oh, Cam…" Her heart bled for the angry young boy who looked out of his eyes. At last, Jayne understood why he was so reluctant to believe she wanted to stay with him. She couldn't help but feel sorry for the woman who had felt that her only way out was to take her own life but she also knew it was also an unbelievably selfish thing to do to your family. She watched as Cam ate a few bites of the sandwich, giving him time to gather his thoughts. A few moments passed in silence before he spoke again.

"When one half of a bonded couple dies the other often follows. They stop eatin', withdraw into themselves. Stop livin'. Eight months after my mother died, my father died too, pinin' for a woman who couldnae stand the sight of him."

She wanted to go to him, pull him into her arms but she knew he wouldn't welcome it. "I'm sorry, Cameron."

"What for, you didnae kill them." He finished the sandwich and sat back. "So, now you know my sad story and you know why it's so important to me that you understand exactly what you're getting into. I didnae—don't—ever want to do to someone else what he did to her."

His jaw clenched with an anger and pain that Jayne understood all too well. She rose and went to kneel behind him, kneading the tension from his shoulders. "I never told you about my father."

"I know that he was killed."

"Then you know the official ruling. He loved my mother more than anything else in this world and when she died he just…slid into a whiskey bottle and disintegrated. He left a note, I still have it." It still hurt, she discovered, but not in the way that it had. Cameron swore and his hand came up to grasp hers, where it had grown still on his shoulder. He drew her around and onto his lap, holding her in his arms. The warmth of his body surrounded her and she felt comforted. "He drove into that bridge deliberately, the same one that killed my mother. I never told anyone the truth, not even Megan, though I'm sure she suspects." She shook off the ghosts of the past, determined not to let them drag her back into the place she had been before and lightened her tone. "It looks as though we have more in common than we realized...which brings me to my second question, the *Dearbh Ceangal*."

He looked at her from under lowered brows and went along with her change of subject. "Where did you hear that anyway?"

"From you, the first night we arrived you muttered it in your sleep. But I still don't know what it means. It obviously meant something to Mary though. She was thrilled when she heard you."

"I bet she was," he muttered. "The *Dearbh Ceangal*...it means the proven bond. I didnae want to believe a *Dearbh Ceangal* could exist because it makes what my father did to my mother all the worse. I told you how we recognize our mate but there's more to it. Aye, we recognize our mates by the birthmark, by scent and by the mental link. The connections that are formed are usually based on purely physical attraction, animal instinct. My parents had that kind of bond...it's taken me a long time to accept that. A proven bond is different, it exists only between true mates—a couple who are a perfect match."

Jayne's mouth dropped open in surprise. "Us? You mean you and me?" She sat up and he winced and shifted her slightly.

"Aye, you and me. Imagine my surprise at finding you at my best friend's wedding."

She sighed. "Is that why you brought me here?"

"No. I brought you here because I believed you were in danger and that's still true. I think that whoever has Nick may be the person who gave James York his information about Jack and Megan. I believe that person is now after you and me. They are targetin' shapeshifters and women who have the birthmark." He explained how he had found the pattern among the missing people. She had to agree with him that it was a little too much for coincidence. "That's why I sought you out. The fact that you were my *Ceangal* had very little to do with it—at least that's what I told myself."

"But how did you know?"

"It was hard to miss. Remember in the kitchen when I let you feel the energy of the bond?"

She nodded. "It was like pins and needles on my hand."

"That was a very small taste of the energy of the *Dearbh Ceangal*. What we feel is a hundred times stronger. I could feel it as soon as you walked into the church for the wedding and continued to feel it until we bonded."

"Well...that certainly explains why you were so determined to avoid me. It had to be uncomfortable, maybe even painful." She wasn't sure how she felt about the fact that her presence had caused him pain.

"No, no' painful, it's no' unpleasant. It's more like a tingling sensation, an intense awareness that your *fìor cèile*, true mate, is nearby." He stroked her arm with his fingertips, making goose bumps shiver over her body. "I avoided you because Ah couldnae even be in the same room without wantin' to be near you, wantin' to be a part of you. Ah still can't."

She reached up and touched the prickly stubble on his cheek, loving the way the light caught its blond color. "The feeling is very, very mutual."

He turned his face into her caress. "Ah know...especially now."

She looked at him, puzzled. "What do you mean?"

"Ah told you that when we started the *Ceangal* that our mental connection would get stronger."

Jayne winced, he had but somehow she had managed to forget that little fact, which made no sense at all. How is it possible that she could put something like that out of her head? *Because you trust him.* "Um, yes, you did. You said you could hear some of my thoughts."

"Usually that's the main effect of the link, it lets us communicate when we change but with it also comes a certain amount of empathy. How strong that empathy is varies with each couple."

He hesitated but she had already guessed what he was going to say. "It's very strong between us."

"Aye."

She knew he was waiting for fear or anger but surprisingly she felt neither, just a calm acceptance. "You realize you are a woman's dream come true?" He raised his brows in question. "You can read her mind, know exactly how she feels and are very good in bed."

He laughed.

A deep, rolling laugh that seemed to take him by surprise as much as her. There he was. This was the man she knew was behind the somber, grouchy exterior. Her eyes stung and she smiled at him. "You should do that more often."

"I havnae had reason to until now, no' for a long time." He tipped her chin up with his fingertips and claimed her mouth in a sweet, soft kiss. She parted her lips and touched her tongue to his, inviting him inside. Desire unfurled within her, warm and heady. They separated, she nipped at his chin and moved to straddle his lap. The robe opened, leaving her naked to his gaze. His cock was hard and ready beneath her, trapped within the confines of his jeans. When he lifted his hands from her waist to cup her breasts, she caught them in her own. "I have plans."

His eyes were hot, pupils dilated, he squeezed her fingers gently but let her hold on. "You mentioned that."

"Take off your shirt and lie back." He complied with a speed that made her grin and she shimmied, allowing the robe to slide from her shoulders. She let her eyes drift over his body for the first time in full light. His hair was loose around his shoulders, his chest broad and well muscled, covered with a fine mat of hair that trailed down over his abdomen and into his jeans. He had scars too, she supposed that was inevitable for someone who had been in the line of work that he had. Apart from the small ones on his chin and eyebrow, there was a thin silvered line across the left side of his ribs and a smaller, rounded mark on his side. Someday she would ask him about all of them and do her best to make him forget whatever pain they had caused him. He reached for her again and she held up a finger. "Not yet." He rolled his eyes and let out an exasperated sigh but lay back on the blanket. She leaned over him and pulled the picnic basket nearer. Her long hair trailed over his chest and he shivered.

"Close your eyes."

His brow creased but he did as she asked. "What are you up to, lass?"

"You'll love it, I promise." *Hmmm…chocolate or honey*? No contest really, she picked out the bottle of chocolate sauce.

Cameron lay before her, eyes still closed, hands at his sides, trying to look as though he was relaxed. But Jayne could see the tension of his jaw and feel the heat of his erection through the rough fabric of his jeans. She twisted the top off the bottle and watched Cam's nose twitch as he caught its scent. His eyes popped open and she raised the bottle and wiggled her eyebrows at him. "This could get messy."

"Jayne…"

With a wicked grin she poured some of the rich sauce over his flat brown nipples and onto the middle of his chest. He sucked in a breath as the cold, thick liquid made contact with his skin. Jayne set the bottle aside. Keeping her eyes on his, she kneeled over him and swirled her tongue over one chocolate-covered nipple.

"Mmm, delicious."

She lapped the sauce from him, leaving his skin damp and glistening. With another quick glance at his face, she kissed her way down the middle of his chest until she reached his waistband. Holding his gaze, she opened his jeans, letting his erection spring free. She brushed her cheek along the velvety hard length of him, enjoying the way his breath quickened.

"Lift your hips." She pulled his jeans off and tossed them away, pausing a moment to enjoy the sight of him spread naked before her, a bad-tempered gift from the goddess. But he wasn't bad-tempered now, it was lust that heated his eyes and he was all hers. She straddled his legs and grabbed the chocolate sauce, holding it high and letting it trickle onto his cock until it was liberally coated. Cam made a strangled sound, his hands gripping into the plaid blanket beneath him.

"Sorry." She smiled, unrepentant. "Guess I should have heated it first."

"Ah hope you're goin' to clean up that mess you made."

In answer, she leaned over him and flicked her tongue over the very tip of him, tasting rich chocolate mingled with the evidence of Cam's excitement. Then stroked her tongue along the hard length, exploring the veins and ridges of his cock. Cleaning the sauce off every inch but the crown until he was panting.

"Have I told you how much I love chocolate?"

"No kiddin'?" he gasped. "Ah think I love it too, remind me to get you more."

Jayne tilted her head. "Look at that, I missed a bit." She bent and took him in her mouth, licking the remainder of the chocolate from him. When she had taken as much of him as she could, she drew back slowly, sucking and caressing the underside of his cock as she did. He groaned and she repeated the action. "Mmmm."

Cam moaned, his body shaking. "Oh, god, enough!"

She released him and he pulled her up to kiss her hard and fast. Her own body was wet, pulsing with the need to have him inside her. She felt his erection damp against her abdomen. He rolled her beneath him, holding his weight on his elbows so that her pebbled nipples just brushed the coarse hair on his chest.

"My turn." He drizzled some of the sauce onto her breasts and just as she had done, he bent his head to her nipples. Drawing first one, then the other into his mouth until they were red and glistening. The pull of his mouth on her breast fueled an answering tug of pleasure at her core and she arched her back and threaded her fingers into his long hair.

As though feeling her need, he caressed her labia with his fingertips, dipping one long finger inside her folds, making her shiver.

"God, yes! You're so wet for me, Jayne."

He spread her moisture to her clitoris and circled it slowly with a gentle pressure. "Do you like that?" Jayne whimpered, letting her legs fall apart to give him better access. He kissed her again, his tongue plundering her mouth as he slipped two fingers into her, his thumb continuing the glorious assault on her clit. Pleasure flooded her system.

"Come inside me, Cameron."

He nipped at her lip and withdrew his fingers only to plunge them back inside again. She moaned and grasped his hair, pulling his head back so that she could look into his eyes. "I want you inside me." His lips quirked in a lopsided smile and he pulled away. Cool air washed over the heated flesh of her body, Jayne almost wept at the loss of his touch. She watched as he reached for the bottle again.

"Tilt your hips."

She did as he asked and he poured some of the rich, thick chocolate onto her mound. Its coolness raised a wave of goose bumps over her body and her inner muscles clenched. She felt it trickle through her pubic hair, over her labia and down over her perineum. When she raised herself up on her elbows and looked at Cam, she saw him viewing its progress with a lust-filled gaze. He licked his lips and raised his eyes to hers as though asking her permission. The words stuck in her throat but she nodded her acquiescence.

He settled between her legs and she watched in fascination as he nuzzled her birthmark, placing a gentle kiss over it.

"Mine. *Fìor cèile*." His golden-brown eyes blazed at her. "Christ, you're beautiful."

He grasped her hips with his big hands and ran the tip of his tongue over the seam of her labia. Jayne hissed a breath in through her teeth and the light, teasing touch was repeated. He parted her sensitive flesh with his tongue and flicked it around, and over her clitoris until she was breathless. "Oh god! Cameron, please! I need you."

His tongue pushed inside her and her head tipped back. She felt the approach of her orgasm in the tightening of her muscles and the throb of her pulse between her legs. He withdrew and plunged in again, a climax washed over her and she moaned.

She felt Cam's weight shift and then settle over her again. He kissed her and she opened her eyes. His erection prodded against her labia as though impatient to be inside. She groped behind her for the corner of the blanket and flipped it back to reveal the small stack of condoms. Cameron unwrapped one and quickly sheathed himself.

"Now, will you come inside me?"

He growled at her and she laughed, raising her hips to meet his slow thrust. She was ready but he was big and her body surrendered to his, gradually. His broad length stretching her until he filled her completely.

"You're so tight." He buried his face in her neck and she felt him tremble as he fought for control. "Put your legs around my hips." Jayne gripped his back and did as he asked and the deeper contact made both of them groan. After a moment, he began to move, pulling almost all the way out and thrusting back in again and again, his hands tunneling into her hair, his mouth on hers. She whimpered as his cock rubbed against her G-spot, her breath coming in short pants that mirrored his. Faster, pushing forward and pulling back, making her blood race through her veins in a heady rush of excitement that made her heart pound and her head whirl. She clutched at him, trying to pull him impossibly deeper and felt her body gather itself. Muscles contracting, back arching, she cried out. Her orgasm crashed into her, rolled over her and took Cameron with it. He thrust into her a final time and growled as his release was triggered by her own. He collapsed heavily against her, quivering and gasping, and then shifted his weight to one side.

"Bloody hell."

Jayne laughed breathlessly and cracked one eye open to look at him. "It was a good plan?"

"Very good. Give me...a minute...and we'll do it again."

"My thoughts exactly, I still have the honey."

He groaned theatrically, clutching his chest. "Christ, you're killin' me!" He chuckled and rolled to his feet, padding into the bathroom. She admired his tight backside and decided she needed to investigate those dimples at the next opportunity.

"Cam?" She heard the toilet flush and he came back into the bedroom. His front was just as stunning as his back and the sight of all that masculine nakedness sidetracked her for a moment. As she watched, his cock began to stir. He cleared his throat and her gaze flew to his face, chagrined. He raised a questioning eyebrow. "We could do it right now, the blood thing, I mean."

"No. Not until you see…" he hesitated and looked away. "Everything."

She sighed. *Stubborn man*! "Right." She wished she had kept her mouth closed. She raked him with her eyes, letting her desire show, and did her best to recapture the playful mood between them. "You have got the most beautiful body, Cameron. One of these days I am going to paint you nude."

He gave her a look that told her he knew exactly what she was doing and pulled her to her feet. "No, it's not me who's beautiful, my *fíor cèile*, it's you." He cupped her chin in his hand. "And Ah'm going to spend the next few hours showin' you how much Ah want you."

Gentle hands stroked her back and buttocks and Jayne lifted her head from Cameron's shoulder. His body was furnace-hot beneath her. She moved cautiously, unwilling to lose the intimacy of the connection, rested her forearm on his chest and looked at his face. His eyes were closed and his lips quirked in a small smile, his long hair was a mess and she lifted her hand and tried to smooth it back into place. She had never been much attracted to men with long hair but Cam's seemed to suit him and she couldn't imagine him any other way. He turned his face toward her hand in that endearingly feline way and she obligingly caressed his cheek. As she did so, she became aware of a rumbling sound and an accompanying vibration from his chest. It took her a few seconds to recognize it. She grinned delightedly.

"You're purring!"

It stopped abruptly and he opened his amber eyes and regarded her warily. "I am?"

"You certainly were. I didn't think lions purred, do it again."

"Lions don't. Ah'm not a lion, Ah just look like one. And I can't do it to order, Ah didn't even know Ah was doin' it the first time." He looked a little uncomfortable at the admission. She leaned down to kiss him and teased, "I think it's adorable, there's a word I never thought I'd use on a man...particularly not you." He scowled at her and she laughed. "And on that note, I think I'll go to the little girls' room." Reluctantly she disengaged their bodies and stood, grabbing the robe from the floor, feeling the heat of his eyes on her all the way to the bathroom door.

She was cleaning up when she heard him call her, a note in his voice that put her instantly on alert. She pulled on his robe and stepped back into the bedroom cautiously. Cam sat on the foot of the bed, red welts scored the skin on his arms and legs and chest where he was scratching himself, and sweat poured down his face and beaded on his skin. He lifted his gaze to hers and she saw his fear and anxiety and even a little embarrassment. When he spoke his voice was strained. "If you dinnae want to see this then you have to leave now."

She took a step toward him not even sure what she was going to do, just knowing she wanted to comfort him somehow. "You're changing?"

"Aye." He groaned and slid to his knees and she raced to his side. He touched her face with a hand that shook violently. "You need to back off a bit...please...Ah need space."

Jayne bit her lip and did as he asked, moving a few feet away to sit on the floor. Hating the feelings of helplessness and fear that filled her. She watched, stunned and fascinated as his hair lengthened into his mane and his golden coat began to grow in. Groans became growls as his body shifted contorted until Cameron Murray was gone and crouching before her, shaking and panting heavily, was the king of the beasts.

He was glorious.

Jayne pressed a trembling hand to her mouth, vaguely aware of the warmth of tears running down her face. Slowly the big cat stood, crept toward her and sat. He towered over her, and for an instant she was afraid. A primal reaction that screamed that he was a predator. Then she caught his familiar scent. Earth and pine trees. She looked in his eyes and the man she loved looked back at her. She threw her arms around his neck and buried her face in his thick mane, relieved and amazed. "Holy shit, Cam! I thought I might pee my pants, I mean if I had been wearing any, which I'm not...aaaand now I'm babbling...but it's just...wow. Gawd, I'm so sorry, that had to hurt."

It hurts like hell.

She drew back to look at him. "Remind me to take some painkillers before I—argh!" Jayne grabbed two fistfuls of his mane. "Did you just speak to me mentally?"

Aye.

"Why didn't you tell me you could do that? Why didn't you do it the first time? It might have saved a whole lot of angst!"

I didnae think to try it and I didnae realize how strong our mental link was then.

Right, of course. "Lord, I need a drink."

It only hurts now because my body fights the transformation. It doesn't hurt after the Ceangal so you wouldnae have to worry.

He nuzzled her and licked her face with his rough tongue. "Ewww! Thanks!"

I thought you enjoyed me licking you.

"Well, yes, but that's entirely different!"

She stood, noticing that her legs still felt a bit unsteady. There was still a half bottle of soda on the bedside table, it was warm, but it would do. Cam watched her as she poured herself a glass. She had just lifted it to her lips when an alarm shrilled through the room.

The effect on Cameron was instantaneous. He jumped to his feet and a bone-chilling growl rolled out of him.

That was the perimeter alarm. Open the doors for me and dinnae turn any lights on!

Pulse beating a nervous tattoo, she complied, following him as he raced downstairs and opening the front door for him too.

"Shouldn't we call the police?"

No, no police. We cannae afford to get them involved.

Cold air swirled around her ankles and beneath the robe as she stared into the darkness. There was absolute silence, even the alarm had stopped. Cameron stood for a moment on the steps with his nose in the air barely visible in his stillness. She waited, fascinated, as he used all his senses to assess the situation like the predator he was.

Lock the door and go to the secure room, stay there until I come back.

He turned and disappeared around the building. Jayne considered following him, she didn't like being told to stay like a naughty puppy. But then common sense reared its ugly head, Cam knew what he was doing. That didn't mean she wasn't going to be ready to help if she had to though. Besides the secure room was a bit too...confining...and anything she could do to put off going there was all to the good. Hitching the robe up, she ran back to her room to dress.

Chapter Twelve

ℰℴ

Henry cursed silently, ears straining for any sound in the woods around him. This op was rapidly going to hell. He had been forced to wait too long, giving the subject time to start changing and now they had lost the element of surprise. The situation had been as perfect as it was going to get, the couple was finally alone in the house and were together in one room. Henry had just been leaving the cover of the trees when suddenly the recently transformed Murray had raced for the door. They had to have tripped some kind of alarm. Now he was out here somewhere hunting them. He peered into the shadows under the trees using the night-vision goggles, alert for any movement. His team was spread out, Scott and Grant on either side of him and Hamilton to the rear. Silent and still, watching and listening as he was. He could practically feel their tension vibrating in the air. They knew as well as he did that somewhere out there was a very angry, very dangerous animal.

To his left an owl screeched and his heart jumped into his throat, his finger twitching reflexively on the trigger of the tranq gun. He drew a deep breath, willing himself to relax. Suddenly behind him, he heard rustling, and as he turned toward it, he heard Hamilton scream. Henry saw the animal, its eyes glowing an eerie white-green through the lenses of the goggles as it stalked through the trees. The lion charged, its deep growling made the hair on the back of his neck stand up. Hamilton raised his weapon.

"NO! Don't shoot!"

* * * * *

Halfway in her panicked run for the door Jayne froze. She had been standing to one side of the window in the back parlor when she heard the bang. Her immediate reaction had been to go to Cameron, make sure he was all right. Because something inside her was screaming that he wasn't. She had never heard a real gunshot in her life before but she knew with a deep certainty that that was what she had just heard.

She forced herself to stand where she was, in the dark hallway and think. Running out into the night wasn't going to do either of them any good. She didn't even know where he was and it was more likely that she would go blundering into the men with the guns. But she couldn't just stand here and do nothing. Cam had been adamant about not involving the police but what choice did she have? Chris and the guys would be miles away by now and even if she knew how to contact them, it would take them too long to get back to do her any good. Turning on her heel, she headed into the living room and picked up the phone, putting it down again with a crash when she realized there was no dial tone. Okay, this was the middle of nowhere, the phone lines must go down often enough to have a cell phone. Besides, Cam was a high-tech kind of guy, he must have one.

It would be in the office.

She had taken a few steps back into the hallway when she heard the knocking on the conservatory door.

"Miss Davis!"

The voice came clearly through the glass and Jayne pressed her back against the wall, watching as a torch beam swept through the kitchen.

"Miss Davis, we know you're there in the hallway, might as well come out. I'm not in the mood to chase you, so here it is. You come out here and we get Murray to a doctor...or you can waste my time while he lies bleeding in the snow."

Jayne felt her whole body go ice cold. Moving slowly, she crept back to the back parlor and peeked out of the window.

The man standing on the patio at the door turned to face her in the reflected light from his torch. He was about five-foot-ten with a stocky build and had a heavy dark brown mustache beneath a crooked nose. It took her a few seconds to recognize him as the fake policeman that Cameron had fought with at the checkpoint. This time though, he was dressed all in black and held a gun in his other hand.

For a few hopeful seconds, she thought he had lied to her and was alone. Then he directed his torch a dozen feet behind him where three other black-clad men stood in a semicircle. One was pointing some kind of handheld computer toward her while the other two trained their guns on the big cat lying on pink-tinged snow. There was blood staining his fur red from his shoulder to his paw. His golden-brown eyes were closed. He didn't move and he made no attempt to communicate with her. *Bastards*! Impotent fury filled her. It swirled in her veins with the fear that they might be lying, that he might already be... *Oh, please let him be unconscious*. A little blood always looked like a lot, he was all right...he had to be. She ran her eyes along the length of his body, searching for any signs of life. But he was too far away and he was very, very still. She had almost given up when she saw the small puffs of white, against the black trousers of the man standing by his head. He was breathing! His warm breath visible in the cold air.

There was really no decision to be made anymore. Quickly she grabbed a notepad and pen from the tabletop and scribbled a note for the others. She grabbed the small, slim, dagger-shaped brass letter opener. Pried up the insole of her boot and slipped it into the hollow cavity beneath. She knew her penchant for buying cheap boots would pay off eventually.

"Ten seconds, Miss Davis, and I'll have them shoot him again. One... Two... Three... Four..."

"Okay! All right, dammit, I'm coming, please...don't hurt him." Cam was going to be really pissed when he woke up and discovered she hadn't done what he had told her. She raced through the kitchen, snatching the towel from the rail on the way past and leaving the note in the cupboard.

Mr. Mustache met her at the glass door, a mocking smile on his face, one arm swept out, inviting her to pass him. She unlocked the door and edged past him, ignoring his chuckle and ran to Cameron's side. She fell to her knees, oblivious to the biting cold of the snow and the bitter wind through her sweater, not noticing that the guns were now pointed at her. The wound on his shoulder bled sluggishly, Jayne pressed the bunched-up towel to it. It wasn't as bad as she had feared. It looked as though the bullet had torn a long furrow through his flesh instead of piercing his body and doing untold internal damage.

She closed her eyes in relief. *So why then, was he unconscious?* The dart pierced the flesh of her arm as she began to turn, suddenly realizing the intent of the man behind her. She felt the cold of the drug flow into her and lifted her head to glare at him.

"It's very fast, Miss Davis, I just hope I didn't give you too much." He grinned at her with nicotine-stained teeth. "It's a veterinary tranquilizer, after all, it was never meant to be used on people."

Jayne shook her head as the scene around her began to do a slow revolution, her body felt heavy and *Mr. Mustache's* voice got very far away. She heard him continue to speak but his words didn't make much sense. The spinning was making her dizzy so she let her heavy eyes close. Everything seemed to slip sideways. She found herself lying on something soft, a familiar scent enveloped her, overlaid by the coppery tang of blood. Beneath her ear she heard a steady *thump…thump…thump…*and everything drifted away.

* * * * *

Cameron moaned, his whole body ached and his shoulder was burning like fire. He lifted a hand to investigate, bumped his elbow on a wall and opened his eyes to find he was in pitch darkness. Abruptly he realized he *had* hands again. Suddenly everything flooded back. Changing in front of Jayne, the alarm, hunting in the woods, the gunshot and pain of being hit…then nothing. *Where the hell was he?* Cautiously he reached out only to encounter walls less than an arm's length on either side of him. There was another wall at his feet and what felt like a grate at his head preventing him from lying completely flat.

He sat up gingerly, hissing in pain as the action pulled at his wounded shoulder, and felt above him. As expected the ceiling was just above his head. It smelled like wood and beneath that was the faint scent of other shifters. *He was in a bloody box*! A large animal carrier, probably. He battled claustrophobia for a few uncomfortable seconds. Lord knows how long he had been unconscious but he had obviously been drugged, *again*. There was no way he would have slept through a change naturally and his wound just wasn't bad enough to take that much out of him. In fact it felt like it was already healing.

A few more minutes of investigation told him that the door latch was on the top corner of the box. Just out of reach of his questing fingers. Cam growled in frustration. Resigned for the moment to his captivity, he concentrated his other senses on figuring out where he was. It was comfortably warm, even though he was still naked from shifting. He could hear the steady drone of air-conditioning so he knew he was in a building. And where there was air-conditioning there were generally people. Why couldn't he hear them? He stuck his nose to the metal grate and breathed deeply. It stank like a hospital. Disinfectant, soap, and chemicals and the faint odor of blood that always seemed to linger in those places.

Bright lights flicked on, blinding him momentarily. Cam squinted against it and saw that he was in a wooden animal crate with a metal cage door. The crate was sitting in a small, blindingly white room, facing a wall made almost entirely from thick glass. Beyond the glass, he could see an equally sterile hallway with a surveillance camera high up on the wall pointing into the cell. *What the hell?* The heavy door opened to the left of the window and a white-coated man backed into the room. Sounds flooded through after him. Distant voices—too far to make out the words, and some kind of machinery, as well as the faint ringing of a cell phone. Cam realized the room had to be soundproofed and the reasons why that might be necessary made his skin crawl.

Scents drifted through the open door but before he could analyze them, something else brought him to full alert. *Jayne*. Her distinct fragrance tormented him and he cursed himself soundly for not recognizing that the *Ceangal* hadn't been missing. When *White coat* cleared the doorway, Cam saw that he and another man were guiding a gurney upon which Jayne lay, eyes closed. She was fully dressed in a sweater and jeans. Her cheeks were flushed pink and he could just detect the steady whisper of her breath.

His fingers curled tightly around the bars of his cage, the press of the cold reinforced steel turning them a bloodless white. Rage swept through him, quick and hot that anyone would dare to lay their hands on his mate. The cat's fury bubbled up inside him, fueling his own. It wanted to throw itself bodily against the door, uncaring that the carrier was designed to resist such attacks. The second man glanced warily at the crate as they passed. Cam growled low in his throat, lips curled in an unmistakable warning. The scent of the man's fear tainted the air. *Good. He should be afraid.*

When they moved out of his sight, he heard the snick of brakes being applied and then the ripping of Velcro as they unfastened the straps securing Jayne.

"Help me put her on the bed."

"Are we not going to…eh…secure her?"

"No, the professor wants her loose. Come on, let's get out of here before she wakes up properly, the drug is only meant to last a few hours and it took that long to get them here."

This time neither man glanced his way as they hurriedly pushed the empty trolley back out of the room. The door closed and Cam heard the clunk of a locking system engage. The harsh lights stayed on, a brutal reminder that they were prisoners. He glared toward the glowing red eye of the surveillance camera, hating the knowledge that someone was watching their every move.

Jayne mumbled sleepily and he heard the rustle of fabric as she moved. His anger faded, replaced by guilt. This was his fault. He should have asked one of the team to protect her in the very beginning, at least then she would have been safe. The cot squeaked and she groaned.

"M' goin' to kill those assholes for giving me the hangover from hell."

He dipped his head in relief and ran a weary hand over his face. "Wonderful. I'll help you, but could you get me out of here first?"

"Cam? Are you all right?" More squeaking and rustling, followed by quick footsteps. "What the hell?" She crouched in front of the grate and he did his best to hide his humiliation at being caged like an animal.

"My sentiments exactly…I'm fine, just a little sore."

"Where are we?"

"I have no idea," he nodded toward the hallway, "but smile for the camera."

"Oh fabulous. We've been kidnapped by a crazed voyeur." She smiled but there was fear in her eyes. "Hang on and I'll get you out of there."

With quick fingers, she unlatched the door and stepped back to let him crawl free. He scrambled to his feet and ran anxious hands over his mate, checking for injuries and finding nothing obvious. There was blood on her knees and cuffs. He frowned and touched her sleeve, but even as he started to question his nose told him the answer. *His.* "Are you all right?"

"I'm okay, my head is throbbing but I got off more lightly than you. Lord, Cam, I thought you would bleed to death." She stared at his half-healed shoulder in amazement before throwing her arms around him. He felt her relief. "Wow...how long was I asleep?"

Cam held her in his arms for a moment, let himself comfort and be comforted before letting go. "No' as long as you think, I heal quickly." He glanced around at the rest of their cell. There was a cot against the back wall with an olive-green blanket and one pillow. Folded on the bottom was a pair of light blue pajama-like trousers and a top to match. In one corner was a sink and toilet and in the other corner there was a table and chair bolted to the floor.

That was it.

He looked back at his mate. "How did you even know I was hurt?"

"I heard the gunshot."

Cam narrowed his eyes in growing suspicion. "The secure room is soundproofed, how could you possibly have heard the shot in there?" She cringed. "You didnae go, did you?" He swept his hand through his tangled hair and began to pace out his agitation. "Dammit, Jayne! If you'd gone to the room when I asked, you would have been safe!"

"And you might be dead!" Jayne threw up her hands. "Don't you growl at me! It wouldn't have made any difference anyway because they would have still come looking for me. They knew I was there."

He rounded on her, snarling. "They *wouldnae* have killed me, they obviously want me alive and they couldnae have got to you if you were in there."

"Yes," she said softly. "They could." She stepped in front of him and put a hand on his chest and that one touch was enough to halt his restless motion. "Because I'd still have come out as soon as they told me you were hurt." The certainty in her voice deflated his anger. She walked away from him and picked up the clothes from the end of the bed, dismissing the subject.

"Now, as much as I enjoy seeing your hot bod…why don't you get dressed?" She shook out the top and held it up. "Hospital scrubs… Have I told you my fantasy about playing doctor?" She winked at him and he caught the garments as she threw them, pulling them on quickly. Cam recognized her attempt to make light of their situation. She was doing her best to pretend the camera didn't bother her. He didn't need to read her emotions to know the truth, he saw it in the slight tremor of her hands and the too bright smile.

She was afraid.

Hell, so was he. He had to get them out of here before they found out exactly why they were needed alive.

Jayne sank onto the edge of the cot and watched Cam start to pace like the lion he was. "A caged one," she muttered, and she was caged along with him. His hair hung loose around his shoulders, glinting gold in the overhead lights. The blue scrubs just a little too tight across his broad shoulders and the thick muscles of his thighs. Even now, her body responded to the wild, masculine energy that seemed to surround him. Not that she was in any state to do anything about it. Her head pounded and she felt shaky and a bit lightheaded from the drug she had been given. It was a horrible feeling to know that she had been unconscious and helpless in unknown hands. Surely she would know if anything had been done to her? She would feel it. She had never been more scared in her life, not even in the last few days and that was saying something! But she refused to show any weakness to whoever might be watching them.

She looked at the camera and rubbed the goose bumps on her arms. It really was a small room. Very small… It didn't really help that it was all painted white, like the walk-in refrigerator at work. Maybe if she thought of it like one of those reality TV shows. The ones where they stuck people in a locked house and kept the cameras on twenty-four hours a day. Except those people volunteered and they knew they would eventually get out. And there was no chance they might lose their lives, well, unless they had a horrible household accident...

"Jayne!"

She blinked and focused on Cameron's face where he had crouched in front of her.

"Did I mention I'm claustrophobic?"

He slid his hands down her arms and took her hands. His voice was almost a growl, his expression fierce. "You have to focus, sweetheart. This is not the time to lose it because if you do, so will I."

He sat beside her, pulled her into his arms, brushed his cheek along hers. *Remember I can feel everything you do, I need my head to be clear right now.* His voice was warm and reassuring in her head. She met his eyes, seeing the worry in their depths, and did her best to pull herself together. "You're right, I can do this...I can. I'm sorry."

He smiled. "It's okay, if ever there was a situation to panic, this is probably it."

"What do they want with us, do you think?"

"I don't know but the men who brought you in mentioned a professor and this place looks and smells like some kind of medical facility. There have been other shifters in that carrier so they obviously know about us, especially now since I evidently shifted back while I was unconscious."

He stood and started to pace again, his anger and unease clear, but some of his words had given her hope. *Other shifters...*

"Do you think Nick is here?"

Cam stopped and turned toward her but he didn't look surprised by her question. He had clearly already considered the possibility. "I dinnae know, mebbe."

Let's hope so, but I don't think we can count on it. The team probably doesn't even know we're missing yet. We have to try and get ourselves out of here.

Right.

"How long have we got until," she flicked her gaze toward the camera and gestured vaguely at his body, "you know?"

"I don't know, a few hours perhaps, judging by the last time." There was tension in his voice and she knew instinctively that he would hate the fact that he would be forced to be on display while he was that vulnerable. But there was something she could do about that.

"Then don't you think that now would be a good time to complete that thing?"

His voice was a low growl that raised goose bumps on her flesh. "No!" Then softer, "No. I don't want you forced into this by circumstance and besides that," he touched her face, "it should be a private, intimate thing between two people, not a performance for strangers. It can wait, we have time."

Aw, that's so sweet…and annoying. Was there nothing she could do to convince him that she wanted him? All of him? But still…it *was* sweet. She kissed him, reveling in the way he responded to her, pulled her closer.

The professor watched the couple embrace on the monitor in front of him, an expression of mild distaste on his face. They were all the same, unable to control their baser instincts. Except for his Theresa, she would never have made such a spectacle of herself. Until the end. Why would she believe he would want to do that to himself? He was a man of science, not an *animal*. And now she was lost to him, but he *would* get her back. If he could only learn how the so-called mating bond worked. He knew the first part was instinct. Get a pair together often enough and it took care of itself, after that though… He shook his head. He had lost too many subjects already, there was something he was missing but he would find it eventually.

Meanwhile there were potentially other, more lucrative, opportunities to be gained from his research. The shapeshifters had some incredible abilities—speed, increased strength, enhanced senses—and then there was their healing. That alone was priceless. If he could find a way to harness these abilities, perhaps even transfer them, the possibilities were endless. Imagine soldiers who had the ferocity of a lion and the ability to heal almost any wound.

He supposed some would ask why not just recruit the shifters themselves? But really, where was the profit in that? Men couldn't be sold to the highest bidder and made to fight for someone else's cause. At least not without motivation and certainly not reliably. But the means to give those strengths to already loyal soldiers... What government would not be interested in that? He smiled grimly, he might even finally get the recognition he deserved instead of hiding away like some dirty secret. And he would still make them pay for the privilege, of course.

The couple in the cell separated, the girl going to lie on the bed while Murray prowled the room. He had taken blood from them both while they were unconscious, but he still needed some from Murray while he was in his human shape. Ideally, it would have been better to get them here before they started to link, Henry would certainly have to make some recompense for that. However, all was not lost since they had yet to make that final step. Perhaps this time, this couple would be the one. He would certainly give them every encouragement...but if it was not to be then he still had other options. He reached for the intercom and flicked the switch. It was time to get to work.

"Bring the male subject to the examination room, usual preparations."

"Yes, sir, Professor."

Chapter Thirteen

ജ

Cameron walked the edges of the small room, exploring, checking for any weaknesses. There were none. There was only one door, securely shut with no access of any kind to the electronic lock from this side. There were no windows except the observation window to the corridor and the ventilation grate was too narrow even for Jayne's slim form. The furniture was securely fastened to the concrete floor. He was making another inspection of the door when he heard the lock click. The springs on the cot squeaked as Jayne sat up and he backed up a few steps so that he stood in front of her.

The man who entered was the one who had led the way when they brought Jayne in earlier. His lab coat was missing and he wore black cargo pants and a black shirt. He held a gun in one hand and some restraints in the other. He stopped just inside the door, weapon pointing at Cam's chest and threw the restraints to Jayne.

"Put these on him, do it right or we'll do this the hard way." He nodded at the gun. "He'll probably heal if I shoot him, but it'll hurt like hell."

The cat rose up within him and Cam concentrated on controlling its rage. He growled softly and the man smiled mockingly at him.

"You can growl all you like, mate, you dinnae scare me. You might be fast but you're no' faster than a bullet."

He felt his *fior cèile*'s uncertainty and turned to give her an almost imperceptible nod. "It's all right, Jayne, do as he says."

He held his hands out and allowed her to fasten the heavy manacles on his wrists. She leaned her forehead on his and he caught her fingers in one hand, giving them a reassuring squeeze.

"Get on with it! Feet, too!"

Jayne muttered something uncomplimentary about the man's parentage under her breath but did as she was ordered.

"Now, get on the bed and stay there. Murray, let's go." He backed out of the door, keeping the gun trained on Cameron until they were both in the corridor. Cam had to force himself not to look back at his mate as the man closed the door and waited for it to lock. She was holding on to her control by her fingernails and her distress cut through him like a knife.

His guard gestured to the left, stepped behind him and shoved Cameron forward with the gun. The unexpected motion caused him to stumble over the short chains binding his ankles and fall heavily into the wall. The collision sent pain shooting through his shoulder where it was still healing. "Just remember her if you feel yourself getting any heroic impulses, mate. The professor says she's the only one you can fuck now so it'd be a shame for anything to happen to her. She's a babe, right enough, long legs, great tits."

Cam's fingers flexed as he imagined sinking his fist—or better yet, his claws—into the man's face. Instead, he righted himself and shuffled forward in silence. He would remember this man's scent and make him pay later. For now, he would try to find some way out and stay alert for any signs of Nick. He willed his mind and body to calm and focused on his surroundings. Like their cell, the walls were painted white and the concrete floor was covered with gray vinyl tiles, cold beneath his bare feet. He could still hear the faint mechanical sound of machinery and a solitary set of footsteps nearby but all else was quiet. Beneath the now familiar scent of disinfectant and blood was a multitude of other smells. Most disturbing was the distinct scent of other feline shifters. They had been here recently but where were they now? None of them were familiar but they were all tainted by fear and anger and more faintly, arousal. It made the hair stand up on the back of his neck in a primal warning. What was this place?

Within a few feet, they came to another door and, past that, another observation window with its camera looking into an empty cell. Another two cells followed before they rounded a corner and crossed the hallway to another unmarked door. Here the scents became stronger, so strong in fact that Cameron came to a dead halt. Neither he nor the cat wanted to go in there. Whatever happened in this place seemed to be focused here and Cam wanted no part of it.

"Move." The gun poked painfully into his back and he forced himself to step forward and open the door.

The small room was set up as some kind of laboratory. In the center of the floor was a reclining chair with arm and leg restraints and a small wheeled stainless steel table. Countertops, storage drawers and cupboards lined the walls. The surfaces were covered with equipment and devices. He recognized a few but most were unfamiliar.

"Get into the chair." Again his back was prodded and he reacted with the lightning-quick ferocity of an animal cornered. Turning to snarl at his guard and grabbing hold of the gun. The man held on but took a quick step back, fear on his face, reflex causing his finger to tighten on the trigger.

Cam closed his eyes and took some deep breaths, reaching for his control. "Don't touch me again."

He turned back to the chair and reluctantly sat, staring fixedly at the wall while his restraints were attached, ankle and wrist, leaving him helpless.

The sound of footsteps drew his attention and he turned to see another man enter the room. He was average height, around five-foot-ten with dark hair and cold blue eyes. He wore a white coat over a pristine white shirt and gray pants. The guard stiffened, almost coming to attention. The arrogance and mocking amusement that had been present in his tone so far was absent as he spoke to the newcomer. It was replaced by an almost fearful respect and a disturbing excitement.

"Do you need me to stay, Professor?"

"No, thank you, Michael, that won't be necessary yet. I'll call you when I need you."

The door closed, leaving them alone and the professor picked up some papers from the nearby counter and began to read. Moments passed in silence as Cam waited for him to speak but when he finished, he merely turned back to the counter and picked up a shallow metal tray. When he sat it on the metal table beside him, Cam saw it was filled with syringes and blood collection bottles and some small vials of drugs. He kept his gaze impassive as the professor wrapped a blood pressure cuff around his arm and switched on the electronic monitor to record his vital signs.

"Are you not goin' to introduce yourself, Professor."

The man glanced up from the monitor screen briefly his voice distracted. "I don't make conversation with my other lab animals, why should I do so with you?"

The machine beeped faster in time with his heart as anger flooded him at the callous words. He pulled against his bonds and the other man sighed and looked away from the readings again. "This would go much easier on you if you would remain calm and cooperate."

"Tell me why you are kidnapping shapeshifters and innocent women!"

No reply.

The professor donned a pair of latex gloves and fastened another strap just above Cam's elbow, holding his forearm steady against the arm of the chair, palm up. Deftly he slipped a needle into a vein and filled five small bottles with blood while Cam could do nothing but glare at him. He removed the needle and pressed some gauze in its place while he undid the strap again.

"Tell me what you are doing to them!"

This time, instead of answering, the professor snapped open one of the vials of clear liquid and drew it quickly into a syringe. *Great, more drugs.* Cameron watched dry-mouthed as he tapped out the air bubbles.

"What is that?"

The monitor betrayed his fear as his heart rate climbed again but he refused to let it show on his face. He drew a sharp breath as he was injected with the drug. It looked as though he was about to find out firsthand what had happened to the others. With a satisfied sound the man pulled off his gloves and moved to lean against the counter, arms folded. His lips curled in a tiny smile as he studied Cameron.

"Your friend isn't here, you know. He was until very recently, just long enough for our little traitor to take the bait."

"You're lying."

"Oh, I'm afraid not." He chuckled softly. "You see, I know everything that goes on in this building. Douglass has already been moved. And when the rest of your little group gets here, my men will be waiting for them. It'll be a nice change to let them come to me."

The lion rushed to the surface and lunged, snarling at the man but was pulled up painfully by the restraints. Cam reined it in with some difficulty, sinking back into the chair. His vision swam and his head spun so he let it drop back heavily onto the headrest. A warm feeling suffused him and he closed his eyes briefly and surrendered to it. When he opened them again the professor was standing over him and he wasn't sure how much time had passed. He struggled to focus his eyes and tried to lift his head but it was too hard.

"Hey! What the hell did you give me?" His voice was slurred and Cam struggled to bring his wayward emotions back under control, fighting the urge to laugh.

"A very special cocktail of my own invention. You should be honored, you're the first to try it out. Tell me your name."

"Cameron Murray." The information slipped easily from his lips and he scowled.

"And how do you feel?"

"Confused." Again, the truth escaped.

"Excellent. Tell me, Mr. Murray, about the mating bond."

"Derv Keel. Fear Kelly." Cam mumbled. "Jayne." He had to pull himself together, before his mouth ran away with him. He laughed at the image.

"Tell me about the mating bond!"

"No."

"Tell me!

"S' magic."

Cam watched the man visibly grope for control, a muscle ticking in his tightly clenched jaw and clenched his own teeth against the urge to chatter. The professor picked up his papers and began making notes with angry stabs of his pen.

"It appears that I may have miscalculated the dosage since all you can do is blather nonsense at me. Let's see what we can do to change that." He stalked away from him and Cam's mind began to wander. He thought about his mate, beautiful, lovely Jayne. All long legs and pale, creamy, soft skin...and that hair... He heard the door open and turned toward it hopefully but it was only the guard.

"Michael, Mr. Murray seems to be having trouble with my questions. Why don't you help him regain his focus."

"With pleasure, sir."

Cam watched as he cracked his knuckles and sniggered at the absurdity of the whole situation. It was like being in the middle of a bad movie. He squinted at the professor who was again leaning against the counter. "Wha'samatta, Prof, dinnae want tae break a nail?"

"On the contrary, why should I get my hands dirty when I have others who are so willing for the opportunity?"

The first blow landed on his jaw and snapped his head to the side. He turned back slowly and smiled at the guard. The next landed on his nose, he felt the crunch as it broke and blood poured down his chin. Inside him, the cat raged and broke to the surface. It fought against the restraints, snarling at the two men. Cam struggled to hold it in check, knowing it did him no good to lose control. The combination of pain and the drugs made the room whirl. Another blow, this one to the mouth, leaving him with the coppery taste of blood.

"Seeing clearly yet, Murray?" Michael sneered.

"Aye." Cam snickered. "I'm seeing your face meetin' my fist in the near future."

That gained him a flurry of blows between his ribs and stomach and face, as well as a few to his wounded shoulder. Blood splattered on the floor and the professor's lab coat and he wrinkled his nose in disgust. Cam felt darkness intruding on his vision. Then it stopped abruptly, someone grabbed his hair and hauled his head up so that he was looking into the professor's face. One eye was swollen almost shut and blood dripped steadily from Cam's chin.

"Tell me about the mating bond."

Cameron laughed with genuine mirth then groaned at the pain it caused to his bruised ribs. "Told you…it's magic."

The professor shook his head in disgust. "Take him away."

Michael looked disappointed but he used a small radio from his belt and within a few moments the nervous man from earlier arrived with a gurney. They unfastened the chair restraints and hauled him up. The quick movement made everything spin around him again and he stumbled the few steps to the gurney. He climbed up, unprotesting, as they strapped him on, and closed his eyes against his various aches. One way or another, he was going to make these men pay but he could bide his time, wait for the right opportunity. They pushed him out of the room and along the corridor while Cam concentrated on keeping his mouth shut. The urge to chatter was still there, indicating that the drug was still coursing strongly through his veins. It was ironic, really, that he had been telling the professor the truth, had in fact been unable to prevent it. *Why was this guy so interested in the mating bond?*

Jayne jumped to her feet as the locks snicked open. When she saw the gurney, her heart almost stopped and she took an automatic step forward before the presence of the gun again halted her. The guard waved her away from the cot and he and his companion, grunting with effort, lifted an unresisting Cameron on to it. His face was bloody, there was bruising already evident and one eye was swollen. She glared at the man with the gun.

"What did you do to him?"

"Don't shoot the messengers, doll, we just pick up and deliver." Before following his partner out of the room, he tossed a key to the floor at her feet. He grinned at her and gave her a lust-filled once-over with his eyes. She waited for the door to snick shut behind them, picked up the key and rushed to Cameron's side, unfastening the cuffs and rubbing the reddened skin on his wrists. He opened his undamaged eye and she saw that his pupil was dilated, his eye slightly unfocused.

"Aw man, they drugged you again, didn't they?" She removed the manacles from his feet, stuck the key in her pocket and checked his injuries. His face was a mess, his nose was probably broken, and he had bruising beginning to form on his ribs and stomach.

"Pick up 'n d'liver, my ass. Bastard." He chuckled and then caught his breath.

"Cameron, my love, you are going to need some serious detoxing when this is all over. What the heck did they give you anyway?" She helped him sit up and watched him shake his head gently in an effort to clear it.

"Dunno…makes me want tae talk." He smiled crookedly at her, then winced at the resulting pain. "If you want tae know if've got any more secrets now'd be a good time to ask."

"Nah, I trust you. Come on." Jayne stood and helped him climb stiffly to his feet. "Let's get you cleaned up." She led him to the bathroom area, sat him on the closed lid of the toilet and filled the sink with warm water.

"Tell me what happened." As he talked, she used the washcloth to remove the blood from his face, wincing at the cut on his eyebrow and the bruising she revealed. By the time she finished, he looked more alert and had stopped slurring his words.

"I'm sorry your friend isn't here." He said nothing but there was an almost unbearable sadness on his battered face. Briskly, she emptied the sink and rinsed out the cloth, then stepped back between his knees. Pasting a cheerful expression on her own face.

"I hate to tell you this but your nose is going to have an even worse bump on it and you're going to have some scars to add to your collection. You're a mess, Cameron."

He squinted at her. "This is goin' to be healed by tomorrow, it's nothing."

She rolled her eyes. "Well, I guessed *that*. If you could almost heal from a gunshot wound in a few hours then this should be easy."

"It was just a graze!" he protested.

"You know, most men would be moaning and complaining right now. Just let me take care of you for a while, Cam." She smoothed his hair back from his face. "It makes me feel better."

With a sigh, he wrapped his arms around her waist and laid his head against her. "I'm no' most men."

"No, you are most certainly not." She stroked his hair thoughtfully. "Why would he need to know about the bond? What could he possibly gain from that?"

"I don't know." *But I need to find out, we've got to get out of here, Jayne. We need to warn Chris and the team that they are walkin' intae a trap.*

"Well then, why not tell him?" Jayne leaned against him and tugged off her boot, quickly retrieving the letter opener and slipping it into her sleeve.

What the hell are you doing?

I have a plan. Do you want out of here or not? Play along, dammit!

He frowned at her but complied, her heart gave a little flutter at the amount of trust that implied. "Are you out of your mind? We have no idea why he wants to know, but I have no doubt it's nothing good!"

What do you think you're going to accomplish with that thing? It wouldn't cut butter and even if it could you wouldnae have the stomach to use it!

Maybe so, but they don't know that. *Come on! These guys have seriously underestimated me, you saw him earlier! He only saw me as a way to keep you in check, no threat. That gives us the advantage.* She marched into the middle of the room, arms spread wide. "Aw, come on, Cam, you said it yourself, what could he possibly gain from knowing?"

He stood, fists clenched at his sides, expression fierce, and stalked toward her. He looked so genuinely threatening that she actually found herself taking a step back.

"You willnae do this." *I am serious, my* fìor cèile, *Ah willnae allow you to put yourself in danger like this. We'll find another way out.*

The door clicked open behind her and she smiled at him. *Too late.*

Our life together is never going to be quiet, is it?

Don't blame me, I was just an ordinary checkout girl quietly minding my own business before you came along.

You could never be ordinary. He gave her a heated once-over and turned his attention to the door.

Chapter Fourteen

ஐ

Jayne followed Cam's gaze and watched the man he had called Michael enter with his gun in hand. He smirked at them.

"Lovers' quarrel already?"

She looked at him and allowed some of her fear to show on her face. "No quarrel, just a little disagreement. I want out of here and I don't see the harm in trading a little bit of information to accomplish that." Cameron growled, a low, inhuman sound that made the hair stand up on the back of her neck. Michael focused his attention on the most obvious threat. He glanced at Jayne. "Let's go, Miss Davis, the professor wants to have a wee chat."

Quickly, before she could chicken out, she slipped behind him and held the blade of the letter opener against his throat. His hand automatically came up to grasp her wrist and she had to fight to hold it in position. His fingers dug painfully into her arm and she used her other hand to scratch at his eyes.

"Bitch."

"Oh, you don't know the half of it."

He struggled against her and Cameron moved with lightning speed, ducking to one side and rushing forward to grab the hand with the gun. She heard a muffled pop as the gun discharged, sending the bullet harmlessly into the opposite wall. Michael cried out as Cam wrenched the gun from his hand and pointed it back at the other man. His hand was shaking slightly and a bead of sweat rolled down his face. Jayne tracked its path with her eyes and met his eyes in puzzlement. The grip on her wrist was suddenly loosened, distracting her, and the guard froze.

"Let him go, Jayne."

She stepped back, rubbing her wrist and put the letter opener in her pocket. "That's not exactly how I pictured that going in my mind."

"No, shit," the guard muttered, his hands raised and his expression defiant. Jayne grabbed the discarded manacles from the floor and quickly fastened them onto his wrists and ankles, she could almost feel the force of his anger flooding out of him. Cameron searched him quickly, finding only a spare ammunition clip for the gun which he stuck in the breast pocket of his scrubs. Expression grim, he grabbed her arm and led her to the door.

"Let's go, someone else is bound to be watching the cameras."

He paused briefly, checking the corridor and she saw him give one last regret-filled look to the left before turning his broad back and leading her right. It took her a few seconds to realize that the lab where they had taken him earlier had to be in the other direction and was the most likely place to find the information he needed. "Aren't we going to the lab? I know they might be waiting for us there but shouldn't we at least try?" she asked softly.

"Nae time."

She looked through the window of their cell as she passed and saw Michael apparently shouting. His face was red and tendons stood out on his neck with his efforts but she heard nothing through the soundproofing. They passed another two cells identical to their own, both empty. "I don't hear any alarms or anything and no one's come yet, maybe we got away with it?"

He looked over his shoulder at her and she saw his face was soaked with sweat. "I need to go to ground...to find somewhere safe...I'm goin' to shift."

"Oh...well, that's...inconvenient." *To say the least.* She reached for his hand, preventing him from scratching since he held the gun in the other.

He snorted. "Aye, that it is." He rolled his shoulders, clearly uncomfortable, and tightened his grip on her hand. He stopped at the next door, listening, and then opened it cautiously. It was a large storage closet, shelving units on three sides containing everything from toilet paper to bleach and a mop and bucket.

"Maybe I should wait outside, there's not much room in here."

Moving fast, Cam stripped out of his clothes, piling them on the floor. "I need you...here," he said through gritted teeth and handed her the gun. It was heavier than she expected, just holding it gave her the shivers. "You don't need to...use it, Jayne. Just hold...on to it for me, okay?"

The change came a little faster that time, though no less painfully judging by the sounds Cam made. She wanted to go to him and hold him in her arms but he wouldn't allow it. At the end, her heart was racing and she had forgotten the enclosed space she was in, too wrapped up in her mate's suffering. When he lay panting on the dusty floor, exhausted, she scooted over to his trembling form. It was still a little disconcerting to be in such close proximity to what looked essentially like a very large lion. But when she looked in his eyes, Cameron looked back at her.

"That's the last time, Cam. No more. Not when I know you don't need to go through that pain."

He licked her fingers and made a low rumbling sound in his throat. *You have a soft heart, my* fìor cèile.

"But not a soft head, let's go." She gathered up the scrubs and peered out into the deserted corridor. "Where to now? Are we going back?"

Cam nudged her out of the way with his nose and started back the way they had been heading, keeping his large body close to the wall. *No, I need to get you out of here, it's too dangerous. We can come back later.*

Later could be too late and they both knew it. As soon as the professor realized they were gone—if he hadn't already—he might start getting rid of any evidence. At the very least, he would be on the defensive. They would never have a better chance to find out what he was doing and if Cameron's friend was lost to them again, it would be at least partly due to her impulsive actions.

"I think we should try."

No. His tail twitched in agitation.

"You know, I am really getting tired of hearing that word from you. Tell you what, you do whatever you want but I'm going back." He rounded on her, lip curled in warning and though he was a terrifying sight, she forced herself to stand her ground.

No. She sensed some kind of inner battle behind those fierce golden eyes and when he lowered his head, she knew the almost submissive action cost him. *Please, Jayne, let me take you to safety. We'll find another way.*

Hearing the plea in his words made battling her own guilt and pride a little easier and finally she nodded. "Okay. How do we get out?"

Thank you. There was relief in his eyes as he turned away from her. *We look for the staff areas, the security will be lightest there.*

They came to the end of the corridor and turned right again, Jayne started to get a little worried about the fact that they had yet to see another soul. The whole building was silent, making her a little jumpy. *Where was everyone?*

As soon as the thought crossed her mind, a door opened a few feet in front of them and the nervous guard walked out. His attention was on fastening his zipper so he didn't immediately see them. She bit her lip. *Staff areas, I assume.* Jayne almost felt sorry for the man as Cameron covered the distance between them in a single fluid bound.

"Fuckin' hell!" The man stumbled back hard against the wall, hands held in front of him defensively. Since he didn't try for a gun, she assumed he wasn't armed and stepped into his line of sight.

"I'd be very quiet and still if I were you, or he's liable to attack."

Cameron growled and the man whimpered. "Oh, god, don't hurt me! I just work in the lab! I was only helpin' tonight because the professor wanted all the guards outside."

Which explained why he had been so nervous, and gave them a perfect opportunity. "Where are the other people who were held here?"

"He...he moved them. To another site."

Cameron's voice was insistent in her head. *How many, where to?* She repeated his questions, watching their captive closely for any signs he might be lying.

"F-five. He moved the last one yesterday. I don't know where." Cam snarled at him and took a threatening step forward and he tried to press himself through the wall. "I don't know, I swear it! He never tells you everything, just what he thinks you need to know."

"What's he doing in this place, to these people?"

If possible the man looked even more terrified. "They're not people, I...I mean, they're usually people when they come here but they don't stay that way. I don't know how he does it and I don't want to know. I just run whatever tests he wants on the samples and give him the results. I can't help you." This last was directed at Cameron himself. Jayne looked at him, unsure what else to ask.

That's enough. He's telling the truth, disnae know any more. He backed off a bit and Jayne felt an immediate easing of tension.

"All right, get back in the bathroom." She gestured at the room he had just left, waiting while the man sidled past her mate, keeping as far away from him as he could. She shut the door and heard him engage the lock and smiled wryly.

Suddenly Cameron whirled to look behind her and roared. When she turned she saw Michael step into the corridor with another gun.

"Good lord, don't we have gun laws in this country?" For a second she thought about the gun hidden in the scrubs she held but decided not to risk it. The man was clearly on edge. He alternated between pointing the gun at her and at Cam who had crouched low to the ground and was inching forward every time the man took his eyes off him. He was a fearsome sight, fangs bared and ears back, tail twitching slightly. She could see the coiled tension in his muscles, his readiness to pounce.

"Don't you move, you sonuvabitch!"

"Well, technically, that's not possible, since he's a cat not a dog." Who had stopped talking to her. All she got from him was a sense of rage and a cold determination and she realized the lion was in complete control.

"SHUT UP!" The barrel swung back up to her and she winced. The cat roared, the sound reverberating off the walls. Movement caught her eye behind the guard and she saw a hand with a gun in it appear around the corner. Then she heard a very familiar, roughened, English voice, its tone casual and almost friendly.

"You know, before you shout at a woman, you really should make sure that none of her friends and family are around."

The gun didn't waver in Michael's hand, if anything it grew steadier. "Aye? And which are you?"

"Both." Chris stepped into the corridor behind Michael, gun pointed at his head and the relief almost buckled her knees. He was dressed in white, from head to foot and a scarf covered most of his face but she would have recognized that deep voice anywhere. Behind him, another man in white emerged, he too had his gun at the ready. The corner of his brown eyes crinkled and she knew he was grinning at her.

"Jayne, darlin', how are you? Mary got your note, she's missed you terribly."

The guard flicked his eyes behind her and she heard cautious footsteps. Jonathon's voice was cold in a way she had never heard it.

"Give it up, mate. The men outside are out of commission and the professor is gone, he's left you to clean up his mess. Whatever he promised you, he took with him."

At last, she saw some of the cocky confidence leave his eyes as he recognized the truth in Jonathon's words. The gun lowered fractionally and he nodded toward Cameron.

"Call him off."

"Jayne," Chris said softly. "If you would do the honors? I don't think our friend will listen to anyone but you at the moment."

She looked at the lion still crouched in front of Michael and privately doubted he was going to listen to anyone. Still, she remembered her mate's promise that the animal would never hurt her and took a shaky step toward him. When she knelt beside him and hesitantly put her hand on his back, she felt the fine quivering of his muscles. It would take very little to push him into action and she hoped that the guard had sense enough to stay still.

"Cameron, come back to me, love. It's okay, he's not going to hurt me." Remembering he could feel her emotions, she concentrated on relaxing her body and tried to keep her thoughts calm. "It's over." He stopped snarling and he moved closer, tangling her fingers in his mane and stroking his soft fur until, gradually, she felt the tension leave him. "Cameron?" He leaned his heavy body onto her knees and turned his head to lick her fingers. *Ah'm here.*

Thank god. She nodded at Chris and he stepped forward to take the gun from Michael. He pulled some plastic ties from a pocket and fastened the guard's hands behind his back with them. "Uh, you might want to check the bathroom too, we left another guy in there." She blinked in astonishment as Ciaran pushed open the door as though there hadn't been a lock holding it closed, leaving the doorjamb in splinters. A cold draft blew out and she saw that the window was open, the lab worker nowhere to be seen. "Well, hell."

Cameron stood and nudged her to her feet. *It doesnae matter, let him go.* Jonathon stepped forward and took her bundle from her. She had completely forgotten she was carrying it and now that it was gone, her arms felt curiously empty. Things happened quickly after that. Chris took the guard and joined Rianne and Fynn to search the facility and "close up the operation", whatever that might mean. Ciaran and Jonathon bickered good-naturedly over who was going to take them home. Jayne offered to drive them herself but that suggestion was met with stony silence.

Finally, Cameron lost patience and bared his fangs at them and they rapidly decided to flip a coin. Ciaran won and jogged off down the corridor with a laugh, leaving Jonathon muttering about the luck of the Irish. They followed him through the deserted facility to a pair of heavy steel doors. Using a number decoder, one of Ciaran's favorite gadgets, he unlocked the door and slid it open, letting in the bitter cold air. She was shocked to see that the sun was only just coming up. The sky beginning to lighten from black to dull gray. The empty hills around them were blanketed with snow and suddenly the team's white outfits made sense.

It was hard to believe that only one night had passed, it felt like days. Jayne took a deep breath of the crisp air, shivering slightly. She was surprised again when, instead of having to walk miles to wherever they had hidden their cars, Jonathon made a beeline for a shiny silver SUV parked next to the building. It must have shown on her face because he grinned at her and explained. "Ri brought the car in once we had done all the hard work, she doesn't like to get her hands dirty."

Beside her, Cameron snorted and Jon shrugged. "All right, so *we* don't like her getting her hands dirty." He scowled. "She doesn't always listen though. Chris managed to persuade her we might need the car to get you guys out." He opened the passenger and the rear doors for them, after a moment's debate, she climbed into the backseat. Cameron leapt in beside her, making the vehicle bounce with his weight. He settled on the seat, laying his head in her lap. As the vehicle moved away, she watched the building until it disappeared behind the hill. She couldn't help but feel it had all been for nothing, Nick was still missing and the professor was gone. Her heart broke for Cameron and Jack but maybe they would find something, some clue that would tell them where to look. Jayne laid her head back, closed her eyes and wondered what would happen next.

Chapter Fifteen

ॐ

Mary was waiting for them when they got back to the house, standing on the front step. Murray House was a beautiful and imposing sight as it loomed protectively behind the housekeeper. As they made their way up the driveway, Jayne was struck by the comforting sense that she was home. She thought of her little apartment standing empty back in MacKenzie Bay and realized that she hadn't missed it in the slightest. How her life had changed in the space of a few days…it was amazing.

Cameron still lay on the seat beside her though he had raised his head from her lap to look out the window. Chris had called his brother's cell phone to let them know they had found very little at the lab. The guard had only confirmed that the professor had been experimenting on shapeshifters but he knew little about what he was doing. Just as the lab worker had said, their employer hadn't shared what he intended to do with the information.

The professor had left nothing to chance, all the records had been cleared out and all of his prisoners were gone. He had even wiped the hard drives of all the computers, though Rianne still held out hope that they would still be able to retrieve some information from them. They knew Nick had been at the compound, the professor himself had told Cameron that, but, so far, they hadn't found anything to tell them where he had gone from there. The guard knew nothing about him, only that he had possibly been part of the professor's special project. A subject that only a very few people had access to. The news had caused an almost frightening rage from Cam and Jonathon but after venting their frustration with some very inventive mental curses, they had both lapsed into silence.

The car drew to a smooth halt and she jumped out, waiting for Cam to follow her before shutting the door. He bounded lightly up the steps and butted his head against Mary. Allowing the housekeeper to crouch and hug him before disappearing through the door. Jayne scowled at his swift departure and ignored Jonathon's sympathetic look. She greeted the other woman, thanking her for sending the cavalry.

Mary pulled her into an affectionate embrace. "I'm just glad you two are all right, it took ten years off my life when I came home and found that note. Besides, Christopher tells me you two had almost rescued yourselves."

"It's true." Jonathon grinned. "They were almost to the front door when we found them."

"Well, almost isn't definitely and I was *really* glad to see you guys. They showed up in the nick of time." She glanced into the house and turned back to Mary and Jonathon. "Will you excuse me? There's something I need to take care of."

Mary smiled. "Go. But be gentle with him, love, the things that hurt us when we're children often take the longest to heal."

She found him in his enormous en-suite bathroom. He had clearly just finished his transformation and was lying curled up on the cold, tiled floor. His broad back was slicked with sweat and shudders racked his body. Jayne grabbed a bath towel and draped it over him, running soothing hands over his shoulders and back. A brief survey told her bruises from his beating were gone, and the wound at his shoulder faded to pink. "Oh, Cam," she whispered.

"L-Leave me alone, Jayne! Ah d-dinnae want you to s-see me like th-this." His teeth were chattering. Ignoring his protests, she stood and turned on the shower before kneeling and cupping his beard-stubbled jaw in her hands. "I love you,

Cameron Murray, you have nothing you need to hide from me." He opened his mouth to answer and she pressed a finger to his lips. "No, don't say anything now. I didn't tell you to force you into some kind of response. I just…wanted you to know."

His lips firmed and he scowled and, for a moment, she thought he was going to argue anyway but he only closed his eyes and nodded his agreement. As the hot water filled the room with steam, she stripped off her clothes and urged him to his feet. He leaned on her heavily, hunched over like an old man.

"Come on now, let's get you in the shower."

"Ah'll be fine in a few minutes."

She nudged him under the spray. "Humor me, Cam."

When the warm water hit his body, he groaned. Jayne wrapped her arms around him, his head on her shoulder and leaned back against the tiles. When the shudders had become the occasional tremor, she picked up the soap and began to wash him. Her hands glided over his shoulders and back and down to his buttocks. Lingering over the dimple she had admired before. He lifted his head to kiss her, his tongue sliding past her lips to duel with hers. He cupped her breasts, brushing her thumbs over the sensitive nipples. Separating their bodies enough for her to work the lather around to his chest and over his taut abdomen and down to his groin.

His cock grew in her hand, drawing a moan from him. His hands slid down her body and she lifted her eyes to his and shook her head. "Don't. Just let me do this, let me take care of you. Please?" She wanted this to be about him, about showing him how much she loved him. Tension left his muscles and his powerful body relaxed. Jayne felt him surrender himself to her and that was a very powerful thing. Cam brought his hands to her waist and leaned his forehead against hers. "Ah don't deserve you, Jayne."

She smiled. "Maybe not. But *I* deserve you."

She cupped his testicles in one slippery hand, he gasped and spread his legs a little and she rolled them, squeezing gently. With her other hand, she stroked his shaft from root to tip with a light pressure, repeating the action until he was making helpless little sounds of pleasure. She felt his grip tighten on her and knew he was close. His breath puffed against her lips, his hips jerking in time with her hand. He came in a rush with a harsh, guttural groan. Jayne felt his knees buckle for an instant before he caught himself and pulled her into his embrace.

Their bodies slithered against each other as the soap from Cam's body spread to her own. He gathered up the bar of soap and cleansed her shoulders and buttocks, caressing her breasts and finally cupping her mound. He played with her clit and slid his fingers between her labia, teasing her until she was begging him to take her. Ignoring her plea, he pulled her under the shower spray and rinsed them both off. He switched off the water and they stepped out of the stall, drying each other with soft warm towels. When they were dry, he took her hand and led her into the bedroom.

Cameron pulled her onto the bed beside him, covering her body with his own. His head still reeled with the knowledge that Jayne loved him. Something that less than a week ago would have terrified him, now filled him with absolute happiness. He nuzzled her neck and nipped at her shoulder and she shivered and urged him onto his back so that she could sit astride him. He reached for the bedside table and the condoms she had left there yesterday. Her hair spilled around her shoulders and her green eyes shone with emotions that stole his breath. She took the silver packet from him and opened it, rolling the thin latex sheath over his erect shaft. Her body was wet and ready for him as she guided him inside, drawing gasps of pleasure from them both.

He reached for her hands and held tight as she rode him, her eyes closed in a delicious self-absorption as she concentrated on pleasuring herself. She rose up on her knees, the tight clasp of her body milking the length of his cock, and then lowered back down. Slowly, so slowly that he had to grit his teeth and force himself not to lift his hips and thrust back inside her. Again she repeated the motion, Cam groaned and his body shook. When she rotated her hips, his control snapped and he pulled her against him, rolling them so that she lay beneath him again. He nipped her earlobe and thrust against her until his cock was as far inside her as possible. "Enough."

Jayne cried out and gave a breathless laugh that told him she had known exactly what she was doing and he silenced her with a kiss. She pulled back, meeting his eyes and whispered, "I love you, Cam."

As before, in the bathroom, he felt the truth of her feelings. Words pressed at his throat, aching to be released but she kissed him again and they flew out of his head and there was only her. All at once, the urgency was gone, her legs hooked over his and they began to rock together. The room filled with the sounds of their lovemaking, the need for conversation gone as each lost themselves in the pleasure of the other. Climax spilled through him, out of him, and Jayne followed, her body clenching tightly around his.

Cameron rolled to his side, holding his mate in his arms and knew he never wanted to let her go again. Since his parent's death, he had done everything in his power to avoid the *Ceangal*, believing it would only bring pain. Now he knew that it would have been far more painful to have never met his *fíor cèile*. He pressed a gentle kiss to her shoulder. There was really only one thing left to do.

"Stay here, I'll be right back."

Jayne's brow furrowed in confusion but she was silent as she watched Cam make a brief stop in the bathroom before pulling on his robe and leaving the room. She sat up against the fat pillows on the bed, pulled the sheet up under her arms and waited as patiently as she was able. When he returned a few moments later, his face was pensive and hope and anxiety warred in his eyes. He carried a narrow, tarnished silver box in his hand. It was just a bit longer than a paperback book and was covered with intricate engraving. Cam sat on the edge of the bed in front of her and sat the box between them. She recognized the engraving on the lid as the same mermaid design from the stained glass windows over the stairs. He ran one long finger over the box and met her questioning gaze.

"I never thought this box would see the light of day, that I'd ever use it." His mouth quirked in a small, self-mocking smile and Jayne felt the first stirring of nerves. "I believed I would never give in, that I was strong enough to resist an animalistic urge to mate. And perhaps that might have been true had it only been a *Ceangal*. But I didnae believe such a thing as a 'proven bond' existed." His smile widened and Jayne found herself smiling back as he continued.

"Then, in the middle of the night, Jack Douglass arrived with Megan and I was forced to at least admit the *possibility* of a Dearbh Ceangal. But that didn't fit in with my beliefs, so I shut myself away and told myself it didnae make any difference." He pushed his hand through his tousled hair and swept her with his golden eyes. "Even at the wedding, when I saw the most beautiful woman I had ever seen. Whose thoughts I could hear and whose heart I could feel. Even when my skin, my whole body was alive with the magic of her presence, my head couldnae accept that she was my *fìor cèile*." He skimmed his fingers down her cheek, Jayne's heart pounded in her chest and she caught his hand in hers. "But my heart did. I love you, Jayne. I think I loved you from the moment I saw you standing in that garden in the moonlight. There's no one else I could imagine spending the rest of my life with."

Tears stung her eyes and she blinked them away and threw her arms around his neck. "I love you, too." He squeezed her tightly, hands stroking her naked back, she felt his big body trembling as he set her away from him.

"Will you join with me, Jayne? Will you complete the *Dearbh Ceangal* and let me be yours forever?"

"Yes." She said it without hesitation but nerves still fluttered in her stomach and shook her body. Life as she knew it was about to take a fantastic turn and she didn't know whether to be scared or excited by that. Then she saw the joy on Cam's face and pushed her fears aside.

He reached for the silver box and opened the lid. Inside, nestled in red velvet was a *Sgian Dubhs*. The knife was clearly very old with its carved horn handle and faded leather sheath. It had no ornamentation other than a blood-red stone held to the top of the hilt with silver. Cameron lifted it from its box and removed it from the sheath, light glinting from the polished blade.

"This *Sgian Dubhs* has been in my father's family for around two hundred years. It's only used for the *Ceangal*." He met her gaze. "Are you sure about this?"

In answer, she took the knife from him and pricked her index finger on the blade. Blood welled to the surface of the small cut and spilled slowly down her finger. She passed the knife back to Cam and he leaned forward and took her finger into the warmth of his mouth. Cleaning the blood from it with gentle swipes of his tongue. When he was done, the bleeding had slowed enough that only a small drop welled to the surface. She watched mesmerized as he cut his own finger and offered it to her. The blood had a slightly metallic taste and she was glad she only needed to take such a tiny amount. Jayne had thought that she might be disgusted by this but found instead that there was an odd sense of intimacy in the act. It wasn't something she would be looking to repeat, but it was easier than she had expected it to be.

Cameron shrugged out of his robe and pulled her to her feet and into the middle of the floor. They stood facing each other, naked, and she began to feel a little awkward.

"How long does it—oh!" A strange tingling began in her hands and feet and swept her whole body, bringing with it a wave of pleasant warmth. Cam knelt and she followed him, feeling the sudden impulse to stretch. The tingling increased as she did so, closing her eyes and arching her back. When she opened her eyes again, she found everything sharper, clearer. Opposite her she saw Cameron had completely changed and when she stopped to take stock of her own body, realized that she had too. The world had opened up, her senses more acute than she would ever have imagined. Cameron's familiar scent came first, soaked into the very fibers of the room, followed by the earthy scent of their recent lovemaking and the light aroma of the bath soap. Her ears twitched as she heard the faint sounds of Mary chatting to Jonathon in the kitchen, dishes clattering as she worked.

Jayne stepped forward cautiously, expecting to be clumsy on her new paws but instead found that the motion came to her instinctively. There was a mirror on the wardrobe door and she approached it eagerly. Reflected back at her was a lioness. Her coat was a little redder than normal, no doubt due to her own hair color, and she was probably a little bigger, but otherwise she was indistinguishable from the real thing. *Wow.*

Cam padded up behind her and nuzzled her face with his own. *You are beautiful, my* fìor cèile.

I can't believe I am standing here like this! She lifted a paw experimentally and watched as her reflection followed. *It's amazing.* She turned to face him, seeing the contentment in his eyes. *I hope this doesn't mean I've lost the grouch I fell in love with. I've become quite fond of him.*

He snorted and she felt his amusement. *I would love to say you had, my love, but I suspect he will still be around at times.*

Good, I'd miss him. She nipped at his ear and bounded out the door and down the stairs, laughing at his startled oath. By the time she skidded onto the kitchen tiles, he had caught up with her. Mary clapped her hands delightedly and Jonathon grinned and threw open the conservatory door for them, letting them dash out into the bright winter afternoon. Cam raced for the pine trees and Jayne followed, savoring the cool, soft snow beneath her paws and the fresh breeze on her face.

Life sang in her veins and she felt she had never been so free. She thought again of her conversation with Megan a few short months ago. Of everything that had happened between then and now and realized... It wasn't always enough to believe in magic, sometimes you had to go out and find it. And sometimes, if you were very lucky, it found you.

Epilogue

❧

Abigail Westford perched nervously on a rock on top of the small hill and watched her little white car sitting in the middle of the road twenty feet away. Its headlights illuminated the stretch of single-track road directly in front of it but all around was darkness, broken only by the faint blue-white glow of patches of snow. There wasn't a sign of human habitation for miles, it was perfect. It had taken her hours to drive the length of the route and back to find the best place to lie in wait. Now all she needed to do was be patient.

The freezing wind nipped at her and she shivered, pulled her black woolen hat down over the tops of her ears and shrank down into the thick down collar of her black jacket. Her breath puffed out in small white clouds in the cold night air and she tucked her hands under her arms to warm them. Her eyes strained against the darkness as she waited for any sign of them, while her brain went around and around. She was doing the right thing. She was. There was just no way she could have left anyone in that situation. Maybe she should have tried another e-mail, or a phone call. Or perhaps she could have shown up in person but she didn't want to be held accountable for *his* actions. No, she had tried to stay out of it, to do it the easy way, but she had been fooled for too long while he covered his tracks. She had no choice but to take some kind of action herself.

There.

The lights of the van swept up the hillside toward her, the incline slowing it down considerably. She gritted her teeth and waited. The other vehicle rounded the bend and disappeared from sight momentarily. When it came around the corner, its headlights swept her, momentarily blinding her, before shining on her beloved car. The driver leaned on his horn, swerving to avoid the little vehicle and she murmured a silent prayer. The van's tires screeched as he fought to brake on the narrow, icy road, skidded and crashed into the ditch on the other side. It toppled half onto its side, the impact shattering one of the lights, and rocked to a halt.

Abby jumped to her feet, her whole body shaking with relief, and slipped and slid down the frozen embankment and across the road. She pulled the tranquilizer gun and handcuffs from the deep pockets of her jacket and clambered up to open the van door. The driver was slumped over the steering wheel and, for a sickening second, she was terrified that she might have killed him. A quick check revealed that he was merely unconscious.

"This is a good thing, it makes it much easier," she reassured herself breathlessly and jumped back down, shoving the handcuffs back in her pocket. If she moved quickly and got this done before he came around, she wouldn't need them. Even better, she could get away without being seen and without needing to worry about finding a way to free him. It was too secluded an area and far too cold to leave it to chance.

At first, when she opened the back doors, all she saw was darkness. Then, from one corner came a menacing growl. Her eyes adjusted to the lack of light and she saw the cage tilted diagonally against one wall. Inside, pale eyes gleamed at her from a midnight-dark, feline face. He bared his teeth and snarled. Abby felt his rage, his confusion and *fear* and it made her want to weep.

"It's all right, it's okay," she murmured, bringing the tranq gun up from her side. "Let's get you out of there, Nick."

The end?

Why an electronic book?

We live in the Information Age—an exciting time in the history of human civilization, in which technology rules supreme and continues to progress in leaps and bounds every minute of every day. For a multitude of reasons, more and more avid literary fans are opting to purchase e-books instead of paper books. The question from those not yet initiated into the world of electronic reading is simply: *Why?*

1. *Price.* An electronic title at Ellora's Cave Publishing and Cerridwen Press runs anywhere from 40% to 75% less than the cover price of the exact same title in paperback format. Why? Basic mathematics and cost. It is less expensive to publish an e-book (no paper and printing, no warehousing and shipping) than it is to publish a paperback, so the savings are passed along to the consumer.

2. *Space.* Running out of room in your house for your books? That is one worry you will never have with electronic books. For a low one-time cost, you can purchase a handheld device specifically designed for e-reading. Many e-readers have large, convenient screens for viewing. Better yet, hundreds of titles can be stored within your new library—on a single microchip. There are a variety of e-readers from different manufacturers. You can also read e-books on your PC or laptop computer. (Please note that Ellora's Cave does not endorse any specific brands.

You can check our websites at www.ellorascave.com or www.cerridwenpress.com for information we make available to new consumers.)

3. *Mobility.* Because your new e-library consists of only a microchip within a small, easily transportable e-reader, your entire cache of books can be taken with you wherever you go.

4. *Personal Viewing Preferences.* Are the words you are currently reading too small? Too large? Too… ANNOYING? Paperback books cannot be modified according to personal preferences, but e-books can.

5. *Instant Gratification.* Is it the middle of the night and all the bookstores near you are closed? Are you tired of waiting days, sometimes weeks, for bookstores to ship the novels you bought? Ellora's Cave Publishing sells instantaneous downloads twenty-four hours a day, seven days a week, every day of the year. Our webstore is never closed. Our e-book delivery system is 100% automated, meaning your order is filled as soon as you pay for it.

Those are a few of the top reasons why electronic books are replacing paperbacks for many avid readers.

As always, Ellora's Cave and Cerridwen Press welcome your questions and comments. We invite you to email us at Comments@ellorascave.com or write to us directly at Ellora's Cave Publishing Inc., 1056 Home Avenue, Akron, OH 44310-3502.

COMING TO A BOOKSTORE NEAR YOU!

ELLORA'S CAVE

Bestselling Authors Tour

erridwen, the Celtic Goddess of wisdom, was the muse who brought inspiration to storytellers and those in the creative arts. Cerridwen Press encompasses the best and most innovative stories in all genres of today's fiction. Visit our site and discover the newest titles by talented authors who still get inspired - much like the ancient storytellers did, once upon a time.

Cerridwen Press

www.cerridwenpress.com